the summer of
Satan's Gorge

by dorothy m. powell

Cover and Illustrations: Kathryn Cole

SCHOLASTIC-TAB PUBLICATIONS LTD.

123 Newkirk Road, Richmond Hill, Ontario, Canada.

Copyright© 1973 by Dorothy M. Powell.
All rights reserved.
Published by Scholastic-TAB Publications Ltd., 123 Newkirk Road, Richmond Hill, Ontario.

1st printing 1974
Printed in Canada

Chapter

1 Black Rock Lake

The bus began a curving descent into the resort town of Rock's End. Through the dust-smeared pane, Lenny recognized the stone bridge with its abrupt little hump. And despite her reluctance to come, despite all her pleading, she felt the familiar rush of excitement. She had not expected the same delicious feeling.

Five years ago, when she was ten, Lenny had approached the bridge differently. Dad's car, fresh off the assembly line, had been a gleaming metallic green. "What other colour," he'd asked, "with a name like O'Hare?"

Too young, then, Lenny had not questioned the source of her possessions. True, there were frequent changes of address. But moving had been fun. A new car would disappear, but another would take its place. Television sets were taken away, but others were always delivered. Only when some men, rolling up the living room rug and carting it off, had left her mother in tears, did Lenny begin to wonder.

You have to be fifteen, she decided soberly, to question a father whose blue eyes laugh even when his mouth is still — to wonder if his explanation, "Change is the spice of life," is good enough.

Lenny's hands tightened on the tote-bag in her lap. The bag contained her allowance for the summer, money for room and board, a lipstick from Dad — and a list of thoughtful instructions from Mom. But one important item was missing: a return ticket for home.

Only last night, Mom had asked with a tight-lipped smile,

1

"Home? Where might that be?"

"Home is where you find it" was Dad's brilliant response. "Don't worry," he assured Lenny. "You'll know exactly where we are in the States. And, once a week, we'll write to you. In the meantime," he concluded, "you'll be enjoying yourself at the Blooms'."

An elderly couple, the Blooms owned a farm situated inland from the shore of Black Rock Lake, and every summer for the first ten years of Lenny's life they had become "Gram" and "Gramps" to her.

Strangely enough, the rented lakeside cottage on the Blooms' land held more permanency in Lenny's memory than any other home. The daily walk to the farm, following a pine-needled path for milk, eggs and butter, had been a fine, steady ritual. At this very moment, it seemed the essence of security. But not without Mom and Dad — not alone.

Easing slowly into town, the bus passed a sign that proudly announced a population of 8,300 persons. Tourists, topped with beach hats and goggled in sunglasses, crowded the main street. Surging into Dodd's, the town's largest bakery, they followed the aroma of fresh bread. Or, in front of the Black Rock Hotel, they lingered at the gift shop window to stare at Hudson Bay blankets, beaded moccasins, and genuine Eskimo Ookpiks.

Main Street, Lenny thought, had hardly changed at all. Traffic lights were still non-existent at the intersection: everyone still waited for someone else to make a decision.

Lurching across the street, the bus turned into the terminal and heaved to a stop. Lenny peered into a small sea of welcoming faces. Mr. Bloom would be five years older — and changed. To a ten-year-old, he'd always seemed very ancient: thin, sandy hair combed over a pink dome and faded eyes set deeply under whiskered brows. Tall and very thin, she recalled, he should be easy to spot. But, eyes resting briefly on each glad face, Lenny found no one to fit his description. He was supposed to meet me, she thought indignantly.

The terminal emptied quickly and she was alone, except for a

2

youngster leafing through comic books and a woman inquiring about schedules at the counter.

Approaching the young man in charge, Lenny asked, "Did anyone leave a message. . . for Miss O'Hare?"

The ticket agent looked up with a frown. "If there were any messages, I'd have been told." Opening a drawer and shuffling through papers, he said, "Nope, nothing here."

At Lenny's small "Oh," he asked, "Trouble?"

"I was supposed to be met."

"Wait a while," he advised. "They'll turn up."

The prospect of waiting on a wooden bench in a bare bus station appalled Lenny. People just sit there, she thought bitterly, between places – not belonging anywhere.

"I think I'll go to the Fish Dock," she decided aloud. "That is where he'll tie up. There's only one way from there to here. I can't miss him."

"You might," the young man replied. "Better leave a note saying where you've gone." His eyebrow pulled up the corner of his mouth. "These summer boy friends can't always be trusted."

"It isn't a boy friend," Lenny replied stiffly. "It's my grandfather." The moment the lie left her month, Lenny winced. Why had she said such a thing?

"My mistake," he said pleasantly. But his look said plainly that Lenny's smooth black hair curving softly over her shoulders, the turquoise slacks and creamy sweater all stamped her "city girl" on a weekend date.

"If you don't mind," she said coolly, "I think I will leave a message."

"For Mr. Bloom of Sentinel Farm," she began. "Just say I'll be waiting at the Fish Dock. And sign it 'Lenny O'Hare'."

The young man's pencil remained poised over the pad. "Sid Bloom?"

Lenny nodded, stooping to pick up her bags. But not before she sensed his instant recognition. In Rock's End, Mr. Bloom was known affectionately as "local colour" – a character who refused to change with the times.

"I'll tell Sid," the young man called after her. "That is, if he ever gets here. Like as not, he's still at his own dock — trying to start that crate he calls a boat."

Lenny didn't answer. Leaving the dingy terminal, she was grateful that her relationship to Mr. Bloom had not been pursued any further.

In spite of the crowded street, the air washed her face with freshness. Breathing deeply, she filled her nostrils with the mingled perfume of land-locked water plants, sun-warmed cedar — and something else. Was it possible to sniff adventure? She smiled at the foolish thought.

Two boys in faded jeans slowed their step to a saunter. One gave a low whistle, but Lenny ignored him. It was nice, though, to know she merited a whistle. "Whistles," Mom always insisted, "are fine for the morale. But 'whistle-bait' girls are a dime a dozen."

The street sloped downhill to the dock; Lenny's suitcase and tote-bag made the walk seem longer. But aching shoulders were soon forgotten as the odour of fish grew stronger and familiar landmarks made their appearance. Over there stood the clump of willows where Indians pulled up canoes and outboards. Directly opposite was the supermarket with its docks for lake-living customers. And straight ahead was the little antique store with — yes! — the same fancy French clock on dusty velvet in the window.

So far, Mr. Bloom was nowhere to be seen. Lenny had kept a careful watch on both sides of the street. She was sure, now, she would know him on sight. Rock's End had not changed. Gramps Bloom wouldn't have either.

Still the busiest place on the waterfront, the Fish Dock had craft of every shape and size easing in and out. Customers bought fresh fish at the tiny dockside store, picked up their mail at the post office or made phone calls to island cottagers. Others, like Lenny, were just waiting.

The noon sun was uncomfortably warm as Lenny headed for a triangle of shade cast by the Fish Shop wall. Using the suitcase as a seat, her back against the silvered wood, she gave a gusty sigh, glad to take weight off tired feet and almost forgetting that she'd had no lunch.

Consoling herself that, at least, she'd chosen a grandstand seat, Lenny watched the dock's activity. A large cruiser, sporting a red pennant inscribed with the name PINECREST CAMP, rocked heavily against the pilings. Its skipper, a sunburned man in a rakish naval cap, was herding his passengers carefully aboard. His helper, a good-looking, blond boy, was stripped to the waist, his tanned shoulders shining with perspiration. He stood with one leg on the dock, the other on the heaving cruiser, perfectly synchronized with the motion of the waves. Lenny could not help admiring his muscular ease as he lifted boxes and crates in and out of the cruiser.

A man and wife with their family of four little boys were gathering their suitcases at the dock side in an effort to be helpful. The smallest youngster dragged a wicker cat-basket across the dock and dropped it at the side of the cruiser. Through the basket weave, Lenny could see the terrified animal circling and crouching, its ears flat against its head.

Then, horrified, she saw a tail snake from beneath the basket's door. Twitching on the dock, it lay directly beneath a heavy carton being lowered by the blond boy.

"Wait!" she screamed, leaping to her feet. The boy jerked to a stop, holding the box only inches from the dock.

To his astonished face, she gasped, "The cat! You'll squash its tail!"

Giving Lenny an irritated look, he lowered the box slowly as the cat's tail swished safely to one side. Then he straightened to his full height — well over six feet, Lenny guessed, feeling decidedly smaller and definitely foolish.

His eyes, she noted, were a warm amber, not blue as she had expected. But his voice was cool. "Thanks for the warning, Miss. But cats are pretty good at protecting their own tails."

"Mine wasn't," she retorted. "Mittens was. . . ."

"A dumb cat," he supplied, with a grin.

Lenny's mouth opened, but the cruiser's skipper cut short her reply. "Hey, Todd," he shouted. "Gimme a hand here."

"Be right with you," Todd said, turning his back on Lenny.

But his departure went unnoticed; Lenny, on her knees, tried to soothe a very frightened cat. "Never mind, puss," she murmured. "You'll like it here. Mittens did."

You've got to stop this, Lenny told herself firmly. You've got to stop grieving for Mittens — being bitter about Mom and Dad's decision to have her destroyed.

"Mittens," they had told Lenny, "is much too old to drag to the lake, far too irritable to give any further pleasure — either to herself or to anyone else." Even Dad, always so understanding, had been deaf to Lenny's pleas. "Mittens is mine!" she'd cried. "You've no right. . . ." Then, she'd broken her heart — right there, in front of them — something she rarely did.

But Dad, turning on his heel, had remarked that he couldn't cope anymore with two weeping females. And Mom, trying to be gentle, had said, "We simply can't take Mittens into the States. There would be rabies shots — motels that wouldn't take animals. Besides," she had ended, "your father has enough to worry about without having to worry about a cat."

They couldn't know, Lenny thought, the warmth of a thrumming body on your bed at night. They couldn't know, when Mom was at work, the joy of a welcoming tabby face in the window of an empty house.

The cat in the basket mewed piteously, and Lenny's eyes blurred. She brushed at the tears angrily as the babble of young voices and the music of a transistor floated shoreward.

A cabin cruiser, plated with the name, *The Scotsman*, pulsed throatily into sight. It drew towards the dock, appointments gleaming richly in the sun, its seats occupied by six people about Lenny's age. With the exception of the boy at the wheel, every head was turned to watch the antics of a small boat bobbing corklike in their wake.

Lenny would have known it anywhere. Gramps Bloom had finally arrived!

2 Pixie Disaster

Lenny watched with mixed emotions. Should she let the tears spill, let the lump in her throat take over, or laugh with everyone else? The two craft were the utter ends in water conveyance: one at the peak of the scale, the other at the bottom.

The cruiser, boiling water at the stern, slid gracefully toward the opposite pier. In comparison, Mr. Bloom's shabby little outboard bounced and wallowed: bow pointing skyward at one moment, doing a deep-sea dive the next. Unperturbed, old Sid Bloom sat waiting for the turbulence to stop, one hand on the lever of the battered motor, the other curled into a fist pounding each dying sputter into renewed life. A soiled sun-helmet sloped across his head and from his teeth hung a curved black pipe.

He hasn't changed, Lenny thought happily. He's still the same — even to the catalogue overalls and the heavy lumber boots which were never meant for the lake. Not that he didn't like the water; it was just that for Gramps the land came first. "Water people," he called the cottagers. "Can't trust 'em. Like the lake — unpredictable."

Standing on tiptoe, Lenny waved madly and his eyes found hers, slitting under the brim of his helmet. Fist uncurled, he lifted it in a brief salute. Then the *Pixie*'s motor, as if relieved of its master's demands, gave a loud honk — and died.

A boy in black swim trunks, stretched across the roof of the cruiser's cabin, called, "Hey Mr. Bloom! You're foundering!"

His remark brought a ripple of laughter from the three girls in the cruiser as the prediction almost became truth. Its skipper,

7

either by accident or design, throttled the engine. The result was a helpless *Pixie*, dipping dangerously and wafting featherlike toward the dock.

By now, everyone on the dock had stopped their activity to watch. Gramps, reaching for an oar, prepared to cushion the *Pixie*'s impact against the cruiser's side. Then, the blond boy, Todd, raced along the dock shouting, "The rope, Mr. Bloom! Throw me the rope!"

Lenny expelled her breath, unaware that she'd been holding it, as the *Pixie*, like a reluctant puppy, sidled safely alongside the pier.

There followed one of those strange moments of silence; the far-off squawk of a gull and the rhythmic slap of water on the piles seemed unnaturally loud. Gramps, standing erect in his boat, gripped the dock ladder with one hand and an upraised oar with the other. Then he looked up at Lenny, blue eyes blazing and face purpled with anger.

He doesn't *know* me, she thought. The answering wave of his hand had been merely "courtesy of the lake." To old Sid Bloom she was probably just another tourist.

"Gramps," she said loudly. "It's Lenny."

His face relaxed and the oar, when Lenny snatched at it, became a nautical handshake. It could have been a weapon of retaliation, she thought, picturing him paddling over to the cruiser and swinging at a few heads. Mr. Bloom's fits of temper were really something to witness; Lenny remembered a few episodes she'd rather have forgotten. But the town of Rock's End seemed to cherish them; like folklore, the stories were told and re-told with a frill added here or there to improve the effect.

He hauled himself up the ladder and seized her by both shoulders. "Not little Lenny! Where did the years go?"

She wasn't sure what possessed her. Lately, it had become difficult to display affection. She was aware, too, of being watched by six pairs of eyes. Nevertheless, she stretched to kiss his leathery cheek, knocking his helmet awry and loosening his pipe from his teeth. Together they clutched at it, caught it and laughed. And, strangely, the hurt at being singled out as different was gone.

"Where are your bags?" Gramps demanded and Lenny pointed them out. There was nothing to do but to follow and she hoped to be able to thank the blond boy for his help. But Todd seemed to have vanished.

Loading the *Pixie* was a matter of great dexterity. Beneath the weight of Lenny's luggage and the two passengers, the little craft sank almost to water level. Sitting gingerly on the small seat at the bow, Lenny prayed there would be no further pranks by fun-loving boaters.

Gramps hauled at the starting cord and got no result. Oh, no! Lenny thought. Not again! She and Gramps had blended very nicely into the general dockside scene, the cruiser episode seemingly forgotten. The only person with nothing to do but watch was the boy in black swim trunks.

I don't like him, Lenny decided. She didn't like the lean, dark face, the stringy black hair, his whole bony length. He reminded her of some kind of weasel, or a bird of prey. That's silly, she told herself. I don't even know him; he might be a really nice guy. But even as she looked his lips stretched in a wide grin, uncovering large, white teeth.

Gramps pounded at the battered motor, spun the gas cap on and off and hauled on the starter cord for the tenth time. The *Pixie* spluttered, coughed — and fell silent.

Black Trunks, propped on one elbow, cupped a hand round his mouth and shouted, "Hey, Toddy-boy! Scouts to the rescue again!"

Todd, rounding the corner of the Fish Shop, staggered with two crates of milk, supplies for the Camp. Lowering them at the dock's edge, he straightened with pursed lips. Whether he didn't hear the shouted remark or just chose to ignore it, Lenny couldn't tell. But obviously the two boys knew each other.

Instead, Todd called, "What's the program for tonight?"

Black Trunks shrugged. "Beach party. Yacht Club Dance. Take your pick."

They were still making loud plans when the *Pixie* came to life. Unprepared for the chattering explosion, the sudden jerk, Lenny slid from the seat in an ungainly heap of legs and arms.

Struggling back to a more ladylike position, she saw Gramps smiling broadly and the dock receding. Todd was bent over with merriment and Black Trunks pounded the cabin-top with a gleeful fist. She couldn't help it; she was going to bawl. She could feel her throat muscles tightening, the hot prickle beneath her lids, her whole face going out of shape.

Mercifully, the wind in the channel blew her hair forward. Covering her face, it hid the misery from Gramps, from other boaters, from the boys on the dock. She made a sign to Gramps — above the *Pixie*'s noise there was no use trying to talk — and swung on her seat to face the lake. This way, the wetness on her cheeks could be mistaken for spray, the screwed-up expression simply a water-squint.

It was going to be an awful summer! Why hadn't Mom and Dad taken her along? Surely, it wouldn't have cost *that* much — three people, instead of two. They had pointed out, however, that she was an adult now, and motels were terribly expensive. Besides, this was not intended as a pleasure trip; Dad would be tracking down jobs, following up applications and getting material for new articles. Being a free lance writer, Dad had said, was tough going at any time. But lately, the going had been tougher with magazines folding and editors using the better-known professionals. "You will enjoy yourself more at the lake," they had told her. "Young people your own age — swimming, boating and dancing."

What young people? Lenny asked herself. What chance would she have to meet any? Living inland with two old characters like the Blooms? Sure, she remembered them fondly. But then she had been little, overwhelmed by a real farmyard with cows, chickens and a barn. Mom should have realized that before she went overboard sewing new clothes. And the cool little stretch-bather with the low-dipping back. Where, Lenny wondered dismally, am I going to wear it? In the duck pond? Mom should have bought me denim overalls and a straw hat!

The *Pixie*, chugging up the narrows, was beginning to pitch in choppy water. Waves slapped at her prow, churned down her short length and lifted her flimsy propellor. The motor sounded uncertain as Lenny turned at the already familiar thud of Gramps's fist on the casing. Great! she thought. The perfect place to stall. Right where the water traffic is thickest!

Gliding toward them was a Yacht Club sloop, and directly in their wake Lenny recognized the cruiser from Pinecrest Camp with Todd at the wheel. She could see his blond head through the windshield. Hands tightening on the *Pixie*'s gunwales, neck stiff and eyes straight-ahead, she prayed, "Please, *Pixie*! No more tricks!"

The *Pixie* obeyed. Bobbing through the narrows, scraping the marker buoy, she barely missed the sloop. But she didn't stall.

Up ahead, an island the size of a polka-dot divided the waterways; to the left a passage led into Black Rock Lake and out through Satan's Gorge; to the right were any number of tree-hung water paths.

In smoother water, the *Pixie*'s motor settled to a contented murmur. The Camp cruiser curved to the left with Todd waving a friendly arm and Gramps lifting his helmet in salute. Several campers followed suit, fluttering kerchiefs in their direction, laughing and pointing. Lenny felt hot with shame; she could imagine the remarks. "Who's the character? What a tub!" Sitting straight-backed, she tried desperately to appreciate the scenery, to become part of the boat — anything to wipe out the past hour!

Nosing the shore, the *Pixie* purred past summer cottages and private docks strewn with languid sun-bathers. Some, though, were alive with frenzied activity: groups of youngsters leaping off diving boards, all wearing bright orange regulation life-jackets. Black Rock, a deep freshwater lake, had only one sand beach on the far shore and water safety was rigidly enforced. Cruising police imposed stiff fines for too-few life-jackets in boats, a lack of lights fore and aft at night-time, negligent motorboating of any kind. Lenny remembered that, as a child, she had often sprawled

11

across her bed with her jacket still strapped over a sunsuit, the jacket almost a part of her own anatomy.

The *Pixie*, making a wide curve, headed for a willow-fringed opening and Lenny ducked as dangling fronds brushed the boat's deck.

In another world, they followed a winding ribbon of green shading to sun-flecked amber near the banks. Lake sounds melted away and the forest took over: the harsh squawk of a bluejay, the indignant conversation of a squirrel, the resounding slap of a beaver's tail. Even the *Pixie*'s wake, frilling under lily pads, seemed a part of the scene. Lenny took a deep breath, inhaling the warm scent of pine. Here, she thought, is where Gramps and the *Pixie* belong. Me too, I guess.

As if reading her thoughts, Gramps said, "Pay no attention to those water-people. Not a manner in the lot."

Lenny turned to face him. "You've forgotten the boy who helped."

Gramps's blue eyes lost some of their frost. "You mean Todd Brewster? He's okay," he agreed. "Like the rest, though. Too much money for his own good."

"I thought he was working for the Camp."

Gramps shook his head. "Just when the spirit moves him. Something different to do, I figure. Doesn't have to work. The family used to live on the other side of the lake until a couple of years ago. Now his folks own that summer place next to the one your Dad used to rent. The one with the fancy name."

"You mean Ipperwash?"

He nodded. "That's the one." Frowning, he thumped the motor with his fist. Then, realizing her behaviour was good, he grinned and addressed the boat personally. "Sorry, old girl. Just makes me mad — seeing what they've done to the place."

Lenny was curious. "How do you mean?"

"Made Ipperwash into a regular showplace. Made it bigger. Painted it pink and built a fancy boathouse with rooms for guests."

A dragon-fly came to rest on the thwarts, fanning its peacock wings. Lenny watched it dreamily, accepting its presence and not disturbing it. Mom and Dad leaving her behind and the hurt of losing Mittens seemed far away.

"I used to love Ipperwash," she confessed. "There used to be a 'No Trespassing' sign where I hid in a bush and watched." She laughed. "Once, I went past the boundary and invited myself for afternoon tea — in my life-belt and bathing suit."

"That'd be when old Gossamer owned the place," Gramps told her. "Never did get to like him much. Treating others as if they were several notches below. That's what having money does. Changes people."

What about not having enough money? Lenny wanted to ask. That changes people, too. Your parents quarrel; your mother cries too often; you move from house to house; you lose your friends. . . . Her throat tightened and she wished Gramps hadn't mentioned money. Not here. Not now, in this lovely place.

In a quiet backwater, the *Pixie* drifted toward a sturdy hand-hewn dock. Waiting for them, rope in hand, was Gram Bloom: starched apron standing stiffly away from her printed housedress and a welcome smile on her face.

Nothing has changed, Lenny thought. Gram's flower boxes still bloomed with scarlet begonia. The boathouse windows were still painted a brilliant sky blue. The path leading to Sentinel Farm was still edged with white-washed stones.

It really was like coming home.

3 A Kitten Called Ringo

Stepping onto the dock, Lenny towered above Gram who stared in disbelief. "Whatever happened to you?" she demanded.

Lenny, leaning down to kiss her, laughed. "I grew."

Gram's cheek was smooth as a petal and scented with her one extravagance, an expensive imported cologne.

The only thing missing was Soapy, the Blooms' border collie. In the past, Soapy had been a part of every "little girl" adventure, Lenny's canine shadow.

As if on cue, a dog barked, the sound reverberating so loudly that Lenny was startled. "That's Soapy," she exclaimed. "Where is he?"

"Soapy the Second," Gram corrected. "The old Soapy tangled with a bobcat. We had to have him destroyed."

Gramps was lifting an overturned canoe. "Crazy animal," he remarked. "Likes to hear his own racket under there. Makes him feel big, I guess." At his command, a small, taffy-coloured collie bellied from under the canoe.

"Hey," Lenny said, squatting to the dog's level and stretching out a hand. A moment's sniff and their introduction was over, Soapy's plumed tail waving in approval.

"Soapy's pretty particular," Gram remarked. "But you've always had a way with animals."

"The old Soapy loved everybody," Lenny murmured.

Gramps straightened out from loading Lenny's luggage onto a wheelbarrow; the walk to the farm was an up-and-down affair through thick bush, then downhill to the other side of the peninsula. "Back in," the cottagers called it.

"The old dog," he said, "was too friendly for his own good. He'd be alive today if he hadn't mistaken a bobcat for a barn cat."

"Poor old Soapy," Lenny replied. "You'd think he'd have smelt the difference."

"Hadn't used his nose for years," Gram told her. "Not for anything — except his own dinner."

They were following Gramps along a path that always reminded Lenny of "The Wizard of Oz," it emerged so magically from tangled bush to cultivated bottomland.

"I didn't think bobcats were that dangerous," she remarked when Gramps stopped at the last steep rise, mopping at his brow and puffing. Gramps too, she thought, is getting old. She lifted her tote-bag from the barrow with the suggestion, "Let's lighten the load."

"Might help," he said gruffly. "Like old Soapy, I'm finding things aren't all that easy any more. Little hills are sometimes big, and all cats aren't barn cats."

"My guess," he went on, "is that the dog cornered the cat thinking, maybe, to play. Corner a bobcat, and he'll take on anything."

He heaved the barrow handles. "If I had my way, I'd blow the head off every last one."

At the top of the rise, the lake breeze cooled their faces, lifting Lenny's hair from her neck. Scrambling ahead, Soapy the Second loped in the direction of the farmhouse, unaware of the view. It certainly commanded attention, Lenny thought; at the very least, a two-minute pause. The farm with its two-storied house and barn had fields wheeling about it like neatly folded kerchiefs, their points meeting in the hollow. The buildings, shingled from peak to ground-level and evidence of Gramps's industry, were a silvery grey-green. To the right, in the quiet bay, the water burned blue in the late noon sun against the heavily wooded land spiked with sentinel pine. To the left, it sloped gently to bush, to scrub and to mud flat.

"Let's go," said Gramps, the barrow bouncing over rocks with Lenny's bags threatening to leap down the path under their own steam. "Don't know about you," he called over his shoulder, "but I'm ready for dinner."

"Me too," Lenny agreed, remembering anew that she had skipped lunch.

"Made your favourite dinner," Gram announced. "Roast beef and Yorkshire pudding. Pudding's all ready to pop in the oven."

"Wonderful!" Lenny exclaimed, and promptly tripped over a stone, her tote-bag jerking from her shoulder and sliding down the path. But it went unnoticed at the sudden commotion in the barnyard; Soapy was barking hysterically, sounding more like a siren than a dog. From the hill, they had a good view: the dog was rushing wildly into the orchard, then wheeling in a tawny whirl of colour to repeat the performance. Squawking chickens fluttered in every direction and the cows began to bawl.

"He's spotted the cat," Gramps exclaimed, and quickening his pace, he left the barrow teetering on the slope. "Soapy! Git away from there!"

"Oh," Lenny breathed with relief. "Soapy's allergic to cats."

"To bobcats," Gram corrected with a frown. "They're giving us a lot of trouble. Just last week a calf was mauled and we don't know why. There's no shortage of field mice and rabbits round here. Unless," she mused, "those two have had a taste of livestock before."

"Two?"

"We think there must be a pair. Earlier in the year, we heard their mating screams." Gram shuddered. "Terrible sound. Gives a person the creeps. I just hope Soapy leaves this one alone. I wouldn't want to lose another dog."

Lenny hefted the barrow. No wonder Gramps was puffing, she thought. This thing weighs a ton.

"Don't worry," she assured Gram. "Here they come now." Gramps and Soapy were emerging from the orchard and coming to meet them, the dog wearing a canine grin and Gramps a scowl.

"This dog's a nut," he announced. "Nuthin' there at all."

"Maybe he scared her off," Gram said.

Lenny was curious. "Her?"

"It's a female, all right," Gramps supplied. "More than likely had her kittens and now she is scrounging about for food."

Inside, the house was cool: green blinds drawn against the sun, mottled blue linoleum glassy with wax and Gram's ferns showering from plant stands in every available corner. From the woodshed directly outside the kitchen door drifted the faint aroma of roasting beef.

Hanging his helmet on the top spoke of a hat-tree, Gramps sank into a black leather armchair. "Home," he sighed. " 'S good to be home."

"Yes," Lenny agreed. The only *real* home I know. She wished she could forget. Why don't I remember the houses I've lived in? They certainly weren't shacks. Most were very nice and far better furnished than the Blooms'. Maybe it was because she couldn't point to a giant fern like Gram's and say, "That's almost as old as I am." Maybe because not one new house held a memory. Little things, she admitted, but with a solid background. Something you knew wouldn't change.

Bustling out to the kitchen, Gram said something about the pudding and that she'd show Lenny to her room in a moment. Gramps followed on her heels.

"Now, Sid," she admonished. "Don't start anything. Not when I'm in the midst of a meal."

He winked at Lenny. "Hasn't changed, has she? Still queen in her own kitchen."

Gram laughed. "I'm not that bad. I just don't want you underfoot."

Gramps's retort was typical. "Don't git your girdle in a knot. I'm only getting something for Lenny."

Reappearing, he held a very young kitten cupped in his hands. "For you," he said, plumping a sleeping scrap of fur into Lenny's lap. The kitten stretched its short length, then yawned, revealing a tiny pink cave pinpricked with white. Fixing blue eyes on Lenny, it gave her a wide, baby-stare.

17

She couldn't control the sudden rush of emotion, the choking tears. "I'm sorry," she sobbed to Gramps's perplexed face. "It's so like Mittens — the way she looked when she was little."

Trying to smile through the tears, to erase his defeated look, she sobbed, "Thanks, Gramps. I love kittens — and you remembered."

Gram had come from the kitchen to hover over Lenny. "What have you done to her?" she demanded.

"Nothing," Gramps answered indignantly. "I simply gave her a kitten. That's all."

"I'm sorry. . ." Lenny began again.

"Never mind," Gram broke in, briskly. "I'll show you your room. It's been a long trip and you've not eaten."

"Not since breakfast," Lenny confessed.

"Well, then," Gram assured her. "That's your trouble." To Gramps she said, "Sid, I've run out of eggs. Would you gather me some?"

Jamming the helmet on his head and muttering to himself, Gramps left the house. I've hurt his feeling, Lenny thought.

Upstairs, the bedroom felt warm; but its colours, blue and white, were cool. Against the window, a cut-leaf birch swung lazily in the breeze, a hanging curtain of green.

Depositing the sleeping kitten on a cushioned rocker, Lenny turned to Gram. "Do you mind?"

"Of course not. But don't let her sleep on this." *This* was a quilted, handsewn bedspread. Gram belonged to the Rock's End Quilting Club; the quilt's pattern was called Dresden Plate. It had taken five ladies almost a month to complete it. "Not counting all the preparation beforehand," Gram added.

Lenny drew a finger over the kitten's small skull, tracing the darker lines of gray. "We'll be careful, won't we?" She looked at Gram. "What is it?" she asked. "A 'he' or a 'she'?"

Gram shrugged. "Too young to tell. It's the only one of Bessie's litter that lived. Old Bess didn't seem to care whether I took it or not."

"I think I'll call it Ringo," Lenny decided. "After Ringo

Starr."

Gram sniffed. "Those Beatles. They started all that long hair. You can't tell the difference between boys and girls anymore!"

Lenny prickled with resentment. Why did older people always buck something new? Sure, the Beatles had begun a new hair style. But what about their music? They had made everything before them sound stupid and shallow. She was about to defend the Beatles when Gram interrupted, "Well, I'll leave you to unpack. Dinner'll be ready in about half an hour."

She was standing in the doorway and Lenny felt a sudden need to explain. "Gram," she began. "Downstairs — it didn't mean anything. . . .It's just that Mittens was put away last week. . . ."

The older woman's eyes softened. "I think, maybe it did. Your mother wrote to me how worrisome things have been. They'll straighten themselves out," she predicted. "You'll see."

Lenny nodded, not wanting to talk but grateful for Gram's understanding. She couldn't know how awful it had been: creditors pounding on the door, the telephone shut off, Mom and Dad snapping at one another. "I'll unpack," Lenny said.

She was folding the last pair of shorts, tucking them into the dresser drawer, when Gramps called up the stairs. "Hustle up, girl. Soup's on."

Dinner was a great deal more than soup. Gram outdid herself: roast beef, tender and succulent, new potatoes sprinkled with mint, yellow beans fresh from the garden, and individual Yorkshire puddings puffed high and golden. Then followed Lenny's favourite dessert — deep-dish apple pie with a fat Wedgewood jug full of thick cream for topping. The apples tasted tart and tongue-tickling, a mixture of sweet and sour.

"I'd know these apples anywhere," Lenny announced. "They're from the orchard."

"Wrong," Gramps mumbled. "Orchard's ready to be torn out. Trees are rotten and fruit is wormy."

Lenny felt a twinge of sorrow; the orchard was crammed with happy memories. It had been a place to daydream with Soapy the First. . .to watch, for hours on end, an oriole building its

19

intricate nest... to perch on a branch, feeling as airy as the clouds drifting above, with nothing to do but enjoy it.

Gram's voice brought Lenny from the past. "These apples came from the supermarket. I was lucky to get them, it was so crowded."

"Tourists," Gramps snorted. "Think they'd never eaten before, the way they snatch things up the moment they hit the shelves."

As if to prove his point, the roar of an outboard racketted about the house. "See what I mean?" he said. "No sense, either."

Lenny, clearing dishes from the table, asked, "Isn't the bay too shallow for boats?"

Gramps tamped tobacco in his pipe; then, for emphasis, clanked its bowl on a plate ignoring Gram's raised brows, her concern for the cherished Bridal Wreath dinnerware. " 'Course it's too shallow," he snapped. "Kids on skis swinging into the bay and out. Do it for kicks. Won't stop till someone's hurt — or the bottom's ripped out of a boat."

Through the screened front door, Lenny could see the glitter of sun on the outboard and the taut flash of the skier. His blond head showed white against the dark green of the opposite shore. Todd! One of Gramps's "water-people." Somehow, Todd didn't fit the description; he hadn't fitted the pattern of poised nonchalance, the uncaring attitude of the others.

The outboard curved in a spray of foam and disappeared, leaving Lenny with the distinct feeling of being left out. What did you expect? she asked herself. To be welcomed with open arms? Into a group of the "inner circle"?

The evening dragged after that. She helped Gram with the dishes, finding out that the Bridal Wreath dinnerware went in the oak buffet and not in the kitchen cupboard; that the mixing spoons hung on a special rack on the kitchen wall, and the pots and pans were stacked in the warming oven. She also learned that Gram's eyesight was failing: sugar left gritted in the bottom of teacups, and gravy spots on a plate or two. It's going to be a great summer, Lenny thought wearily.

Dishes done, Gram settled in her usual corner of the parlour, seated in a mustard-coloured chair and getting out a petit-point knitting bag. Gramps snored softly in the black leather chair, enjoying an after dinner nap.

"There're some magazines, dear," Gram whispered. "If you'd like to look at them."

The magazines, mostly back issues of the *National Geographic*, were interesting, but not enough to hold Lenny's interest for very long. There were also some church publications. Leafing listlessly through the pages, Lenny could hear the evening murmur of trees and the sleepy chuckle of birds; then the sweet, watery sound of voices singing in harmony drifted through the evening air.

"Somebody's happy," Gram remarked. "Pinecrest Camp, probably. Usually they have a bonfire and wiener roast every weekend."

"Maybe it's the Yacht Club dance," Lenny suggested. "The water-people — having a ball." She hadn't meant to put it quite that way and Gram's eyes left her knitting.

"I hope you're not going to be lonely, my dear."

Lenny stood up abruptly, the magazine sliding from her lap and Gramps wakening with a grunt.

"Time for bed?" he mumbled.

Bed! Lenny thought. At 10 o'clock on a Saturday night?

"I think I'll go outside," she decided aloud. "For a little walk."

"Don't go far," Gram warned. "You're not used to the bush. It's easy to get turned around."

Lenny couldn't get out of the house fast enough, couldn't resist slamming the screen door. Closing her ears to Gramps's shouted advice, "Don't go near the orchard. That cat might still be there," she stumbled down the flower-lined walk with its whitewashed stones and pushed through the picket gate. Eyes adjusting to the night, she saw Soapy sauntering from the barn with a short "wuff" of welcome.

The barnyard's centre was a velvet hollow, its sides shadowed black by outbuildings, tall trees and climbing slopes. Overhead the stars clustered thickly, making a canopy of glitter. Lenny stooped to pick up a stick, and Soapy danced at her feet.

"Want to play?" she asked, and threw it into the shadows, watching him race after it, hearing the scrabble of paws while he searched. Then he proudly brought it back.

"Know something?" she said, rewarding him with a pat. "I want to play, too. But I guess there's only us."

When she returned, the kitten had taken up residence in Lenny's bedroom. In true catty fashion, Ringo had decided that bedtime was playtime, clawing his (or her) way onto the bed, whirling crazily after his (or her) tail, and generally being a nuisance. Finally, sitting partially propped up with a pillow, Lenny reached for the bright-eyed disturbance.

"You," she said, fondly, "are a kooky cat." Under her hands, the small body relaxed, curling ball-like and making remarkably large purrs. The sound was reminiscent of Mittens, and with it, Lenny's resentment, her fear of the future, slipped away into sleep.

4 The Bet

Lenny wakened to the sparkle of sun on water and the dappled movement of light and shadow cast by the birch at her window. She noticed that Ringo had removed his furry presence. She decided on a sex for the kitten. After all, she couldn't keep calling it a "he-she." With the decision came another more important one: no more feelings of inferiority; no more dwelling on past grey days.

The day was cloudless. A sailboat drifted petal-like on the lake, its sail a splash of scarlet on the blue. Coloured sails were usually sported only for the Annual Yacht Club Race; the event could not be far off.

A loud "miaow" from the bottom of the stairs indicated that Ringo, despite his short legs, had managed the steep descent.

In the kitchen, Gram remarked, "Don't tell me that's the kitten!"

Gramps chuckled. "He'll have to hustle some — to catch up with the size of his voice."

Lenny hurried into her jeans and ran a brush through her hair — which didn't look too terrible considering she'd forgotten to wash it — and noted with satisfaction that her eyes matched the stripes of her top, clear and brightly blue. Nobody would ever guess she'd sobbed into her pillow for part of the night. Then, following the aroma of frying bacon and perking coffee, she went downstairs.

"Good afternoon," Gramps greeted her. Lenny's eyes flew to the clock. It was only 9.30!

"Pay no attention," Gram said. "Every morning, he cracks the same old joke." She placed a bowl of steaming oatmeal in front of Lenny and moved closer a dish of brown sugar.

Lenny looked at it dubiously. "I don't think. . . ." she began. "For me, toast and coffee is enough."

"Nonsense," Gramps told her. "Eat up. You look like you need it. Nuthin' but skin and bone."

Gram stood back, eyeing Lenny's tight jeans. "Not skinny," she said. "Just a mite too slender."

Rather than argue, Lenny dipped her spoon into the porridge, feeling a bit like one of Gramps's calves being sized up for sale. When the bowl was empty, she looked at it with surprise. "It must be the air," she laughed.

Gram nodded complacently. "You get outside and breathe in some more. Mornings at the lake are too nice to miss."

Assured that she would have all month to help with the dishes, Lenny stayed only long enough to give Ringo a saucer of cream. All through breakfast, the kitten had curved about her ankles alternately mewing and purring. Not as musical as his namesake, Lenny thought, but demanding an audience just the same.

Gram was so right; mornings at the lake were really something to see. The air, almost effervescent, bubbled into the nostrils, a heady mixture of woods and water, of barnyard manure and sun on flowers.

Gramps knelt in the barn doorway, holding a black and white calf with one arm, applying ointment to its neck with his free hand.

Coming nearer, Lenny grimaced. The open wounds were not large, but swollen and festering. "Ugh!" she said. "Did a bobcat do that?"

Gramps nodded. "Not very pretty, huh? Tried to go for the jugular, I guess. If Soapy hadn't scared the cat off, this little guy would've been a goner."

Lenny shuddered, feeling a little sick. "I didn't think that bobcats were so big."

"They aren't," Gramps replied. "Fifteen — twenty pounds,

is all. Twenty pounds, though, is considered big." He dipped into the can of ointment, smearing it gently on the calf's shoulder. "Can't figure why the cat's bothering the livestock. Unless there's a shortage of field mice."

The calf bawled piteously and Lenny looked away. "I think I'll go down to the dock," she said. "If Gram wants me, that's where I'll be."

"Come on, Soapy," she called, running quickly down the path, the dog at her heels.

This dock was the old one, silvered with age, its planks split in places where winter ice had heaved the underpinnings. As Lenny recalled, the bay was rarely used anymore, the sandbar at its entrance making navigation too tricky for boats of any draught. Todd and the rest, she thought, must be lame-brains to try water-skiing in here.

Stretched on her stomach, arms cradling her head, she felt the sun's warmth on her back. Through a crack in the planks, algae-flecked water lifted and fell — lifted and fell. I just got out of bed, she thought drowsily.

The roar of a motor and a sudden icy spray jerked Lenny to her knees, breath sucked in with shock. The boat, curving round the bay, had Black Trunks at the wheel and another boy shouting instructions to the skier in its wake. At the end of the towline, Lenny recognized Todd.

Completing the bay's small circle, narrowly missing the far shore, he skimmed gracefully toward the dock, one arm raised in greeting. Lenny waved in glad response. I *am* glad, she thought. Who wouldn't be?

Surging past in a sparkle of foam, Todd's tanned body glistened with spray. Head thrown back and smile a broad, white flash, he was every blond male Lenny had ever admired. And he has made a point of coming here to meet me, she thought. I *think* that he has.

The next moment, she was sure. Releasing the towline, Todd sank slowly a few yards from the dock. As the motor idled quietly, Black Trunks called, "Don't forget the skis." Surfacing,

Todd corralled both skis, pushing them toward the boat. Then with clean powerful strokes, he turned back to the dock — and to Lenny.

"One other thing," Black Trunks shouted. "Don't forget I've got money on you."

What did that mean? Lenny wondered uneasily. But Todd paid no attention. Clinging to the ancient ladder with one hand, he brushed at his eyes with the other. This morning, they were more green than amber, Lenny thought.

"Hi!" he said.

"Hi," she said back — and there was nothing more to say. Why, she asked herself with honest disgust, don't I ever say anything brilliant? The way they do in books — or on television? "Good looks," she could hear her mother saying, "mean absolutely nothing if there's no personality to back them up."

Todd was laughing up at her. "Well," he asked "Aren't you going to ask me ashore?"

"Oh," she said. "Yes!" and held out a helping hand. His grasp was cold and wet: strong fingers twining about her own. The ladder creaked under his weight.

"It's old," she began. "Be care...." The warning went unfinished. The rung snapped, his hand tightened, and he was flailing backward. With no time to straighten into a dive, she could only wrench herself free — and sail awkwardly over his head.

The blue water of the bay came up to meet her. It jarred her stomach with a solid smack, jetted the breath from her mouth — and filled the vacuum. Lenny came up choking for air, and fighting mad.

Todd's head emerged inches away. "You idiot!" she screamed. "You rotten bum!" She pushed his laughing face underwater. The effort cost her another gulp of the bay, and she surfaced coughing and spitting.

I've forgotten how to swim! she thought, panic-stricken, arms windmilling and legs thrashing heavily with sneakers like leaden weights. Above her pounding heart, Todd's voice came loud and hollow-sounding. "Hey! Take is easy. Stop struggling."

One of the commands she must have obeyed. They were clinging to the ladder, his arm tight about her waist and his face serious. "I'm sorry. I didn't know you couldn't swim."

"I can," she snapped. "I just haven't done any recently."

"You don't have to believe me," he muttered reproachfully. "But, I didn't dunk you on purpose."

Lenny searched his face. He *was* sorry — and the ladder *was* old. "It's I who should apologize," she said, suddenly aware of the sight she must be making, pushing back string-wet hair and plucking anxiously at sodden clothes.

His arm remained firmly about her waist, seeping warmth through her wet top. From the bay came Black Trunk's voice. "Fast work, Toddy-boy. Fast work."

Pulling sharply away, Lenny said, "I'd better change," and started up the path. Todd followed, his wet feet padding on grass. Lenny questioned him with raised brows.

"Eggs," he explained. "I've come for our weekly supply."

"Oh," she said coolly, wondering if he always came by such a difficult route. "Gram will look after you."

"Your grandmother?"

"Well. . ." Lenny began. He wouldn't understand, she decided. Even in dripping swim trunks, Todd looked poised. He had that certain air: the sure knowledge that he would be accepted no matter what the circumstances. With scads of money, a background of security, and good looks, what boy would understand her real reason for calling the Blooms "Gram" and "Gramps"? Lenny wasn't sure of her own reasons. It just makes me feel good, she decided — like being under an electric blanket on a wild winter's night, feeling the warmth spread from toes to shoulder.

Todd was waiting for her answer. Well, he isn't going to get one, she decided. He would want to know more: Where do you live? What does your father do? Your school? Your grade? How does one confess that one's father is a lovable but screwy Irishman. "He's a writer," she could hear herself saying. "But he doesn't sell much. At least, not enough." What would a boy like Todd know about bad credit ratings — so shaky that there wasn't one good store left to shop in! How do you say, "I don't live *anywhere*!"

Lenny quickened her step; she mustn't start bawling again. It was becoming a habit. Once, she knew a girl named Erna who bawled at the drop of a hat. A one-time friend, "Ern" had cut loose from home and hit the road for six months. During that time, she had managed to experience just about the whole scene before her parents caught up with her. She also managed to land in hospital, a complete wreck — and, she looked it. At first Lenny had felt envy — what was it like, at fourteen, to have seen and done everything! — then, pity. It had made her feel "strange" just to be with Erna.

A low-lying cedar fanned across the path. Lenny broke through it, letting the branch slap rudely back. "You usually this chatty?" Todd asked.

He was at her side, hurrying to keep up.

"I'm wet," she informed him, smacking viciously at a mosquito on her arm.

He grinned down at her. "No kiddin'?" His eyes slowly travelled her whole wet length. Lenny felt the anger boiling up within her.

"Aw, c'mon," he urged. "Cut the mad."

"Who's mad?" she asked with bright bitterness, and started to run, hearing the slosh of water between her toes, aware of her hair flapping ropily about her shoulders. I must look like a clown, she thought.

Lenny had hoped she could make it up to the bedroom without any explanation. But in the living room, Gram was bending over the ferns, testing the soil with her forefinger.

To the older woman's look of astonishment, Lenny blurted, "I fell in. I'll mop up the puddles when I come down."

"Oh, my!" Gram exclaimed. But Todd's appearance at the veranda door stopped any further questions.

"My fault, Mrs. Bloom," Lenny heard him say. "She was

helping me onto the dock and the ladder gave way." He laughed. "Since I'm here, I may as well pick up the eggs."

Gram sounded confused. "Yes. Oh, eggs! I should've warned Lenny about the dock. Do come in, Todd."

"I'd better stay out here. I'll drip all over your floors."

Smooth, Lenny thought. He's really smooth. Knows how to act with everybody; good manners, thoughtful with older people. Yet, there was something wrong. "Fast work, Toddy-boy," Black Trunks had shouted. And something about money.

Pulling the wet jersey over her head, Lenny jerked at it savagely, dropping it on Gram's precious quilt, then snatching it off. The boys have a bet of some kind, she decided furiously. I'm Lenny O'Hare, the new girl, that old hayseed Sid Bloom's granddaughter — and easy pickings! Well, she wasn't going to give them the laughs they expected.

Facing herself in the mirror, she saw the black scowl: full lips pressed into a thin, unattractive line. She smoothed out the frown and made an effort to smile. But nothing could be done about the high splash of colour on each cheekbone. It always appeared when she was angry. Her hair seemed insistent about curling: ends perking upward and bangs rippling. Her only satisfaction was the snug fit of her black shorts and the vivid blue splash of her top.

"Ready, Lenny?" Gram called. "Todd is waiting."

"Waiting? What for?"

"He wants to walk you over to Ipperwash."

Reaching for a kerchief on the chair back, Lenny noted a small hollow where Ringo had slept on the cushion. "Tell Todd 'thanks,'" she called. "But not today."

Gram's steps were on the stairs. "You should, dear," she said, and Lenny detected the unspoken message. A stroke of good fortune, it said, to be with other young people — especially those in Todd's social bracket.

In the doorway, Gram stood with creased forehead and fingers making a pleat in her starched apron. "You're all right, aren't you, dear?"

Todd's voice boomed up the stairwell. "Thought you'd like to see Ipperwash again. Mrs. Bloom says you remember it as a kid."

Gram nodded. "You'd like that, wouldn't you?"

Its hopeless, Lenny thought. Todd is one of Gram's customers. And being unfriendly to customers is hardly the way to sell eggs.

Todd was waiting in the kitchen, two egg cartons under each arm. Greeting Lenny with a broad smile, he held out a couple of boxes. "Here," he said. "You can help tote."

Directly behind her on the path, he gave a low whistle intended only for Lenny's ears. "Nice," he remarked. "Verr-ee nice!"

She was about to swing on him to tell him she couldn't care less about seeing Ipperwash, when Gram called from the back porch. "Lenny! Keep an eye open for Ringo. He seems to have disappeared."

"Ringo?"

"He can't have gone far," Gram assured her. "Likely he's back in the barn with Bessie."

Lenny turned sharply off the path. "I'll look," she said, and collided with Todd, the four cartons of eggs in danger of being scrambled.

"Who's Ringo?" he asked. "And what about our walk in the woods?"

"My kitten," Lenny snapped, not caring if it sounded childish. "Your walk in the woods'll have to wait." Ringo, she wanted to say, can't wait. He's special because he's mine — about the only thing I really own!

"A cat!" Todd exclaimed. "Is that all?"

Lenny shot him an angry glance. "You don't like cats," she accused.

He shrugged. "Cats are creepy. You never know where they are. Like now, for instance."

His eyes, no longer green, were amber and flecked with leaf-shadow from the apple branches overhead. Lenny was tempted to tell him that he must be part cat, himself; his eyes and disposition were just as unpredictable.

Instead, she said, "Don't bother waiting. It might take a while to find him."

"I'll help look," he offered promptly and deposited the eggs on a tree stump. How about the barn?" he suggested. " 'S nice and dark in there."

Gramp's cackle came from the barn's interior. "May be dark, son," he hooted. "But t'aint lonely."

Lenny flushed with embarrassment. "You take the barn," she muttered. "I'll take the orchard."

Entering the first line of crooked old trees, Lenny heard Todd's remark to Soapy who was greeting him with a wide collie grin. "At least, somebody's friendly," he said.

Stumbling over clotted earth whiskered with sawgrass, Lenny realised her thoughts were as tangled as the knotted limbs above. A crazy pattern of leaf and branch, they blotted out the sky's happy blue.

5 Just a Scratch

The orchard was not as Lenny remembered it. Five years ago, maybe seven, the trees had seemed gigantic, like the pillars of a hall in some dreamland castle. The leaves had been an emerald brocade, the apples like hanging gems.

Now it was only a bunch of sad old trees leaning against one another for support, their gnarled trunks scabbed with mould and crawling with ants.

Lenny shuddered as a spider's web brushed her face, clinging stickily. Its small, leggy tenant scrambled on a floating strand, then disappeared. "I've busted its home, Mummy," she could remember telling her mother. How long ago was that?

"Don't worry, love," Mom had said. "The spider will make another home — bigger and more beautiful than the last." Mom had been young then, with a sparkling kind of prettiness. But the lovely legend of the spider had faded. And so has my mother, Lenny thought. She has given up: not trying anymore, not even hoping. Dad doesn't believe what he's saying either: that every editor will jump at his next article, that the bank will ease off on the strength of it, that some other store will welcome the O'Hare's credit.

A discarded apple crate leaned against a tree and, straightening it, Lenny sat down. This time Todd had not followed her. After all, she thought bitterly, I hardly encouraged his friendship.

But no matter how she looked at it, she could not ignore Black Trunk's unflattering bet shouted across the water. "If Ringo hadn't disappeared," she mused aloud, "I'd know by now whether Todd is for real or not."

Lenny sat up on the crate. Ringo! I'm supposed to be looking for a kitten. Was that a kitten's mew? A movement deep down the lane of trees? At the lane's end was a log fence, barely visible beneath wild grape and tented with young birch.

Lenny listened, rising slowly to her feet, aware of being cautious and not knowing why. Why should anything be wrong, she wondered. Kittens do wander, don't they? But Ringo was so tiny and the only one of Bessie's litter to survive. Lenny's eyes travelled the way she had come, over clumps of claylike earth, each one a real obstacle for a baby like Ringo. "Don't let him be hurt," she prayed, "or dying."

The orchard smelled musty. The light, a stagnant green, seemed to move like liquid when a breeze stirred the leaves. She could hear Todd and Gramps in conversation, their voices mingling with the drone of insects, punctuated by Soapy's staccato bark. As he had promised, Todd must have searched the barn; obviously Ringo was not there. Not aware that she had come to any decision concerning Todd — the fact that she had expected him to carry out a promise — Lenny felt a lift in spirits. He had not left without her.

There it was again — a plaintive mew coming from the tangle of wild grape. She glimpsed a small, tabby face and a flurry of movement in the leaf and shadow! Knowing the ways of cats, Lenny slowed to a stroll pretending indifference. Even kittens of Ringo's tender age liked to play "hunter and the hunted": lying motionless in concealment, stalking a blown leaf or twig, bellying through long grass after imaginary prey.

Stooping to pick a foxtail, feigning interest in everything but the grape thicket, Lenny moved closer. Little devil! she thought. Imagine coming all this distance just to play "cops and robbers."

A few feet from the vine, Lenny bent on one knee to tighten a shoelace, deliberately trailing the foxtail with her free hand. A moment went by, then another. But Ringo made no response to the bait. That's funny, Lenny thought. He isn't *that* smart! A prickling began at the back of her neck. Dropping all pretense she peered into the lacery of leaves.

Ringo was there, all right — but hanging helpless in his mother's mouth. Bessie's eyes, a piercing yellow, glared into Lenny's. Ringed with black on a matte of white, they glowed in the thicket's gloom — ferocious enough to stop any further prying.

"Okay," Lenny whispered. "I get the message." Gram had given the impression that Bessie was a scrawny old barn cat. But Bessie was a beauty, a huge tabby with the face markings of a tiger. Ready to act like one, too, Lenny thought, if I make one false step.

"Simmer down," she said aloud. "I won't take your kitten." She reached to part the vines. The movement brought a bubbling snarl and the razor slice of raking claws. Stunned, Lenny saw the cat's slithering retreat, Ringo still dangling from her mouth. Feeling suddenly sick, she watched blood welling freely from deep parallel wounds down the whole length of her arm.

"Gramps!" she called, weakly. "Todd!"

Soapy arrived first, a taffy-coloured fury streaking into the orchard barking hysterically. Todd followed close on the dog's heels with Gramps puffing in the rear. Eyes wide at the wet redness blotting Lenny's clothes, he exclaimed, "Good Lord! What happened?"

"Bessie," Lenny babbled. "She attacked me."

Gramps, with chest heaving and breath whistling past the pipe in his teeth, retorted, "Bessie! Bessie wouldn't hurt a fly!" Then pushing Todd aside, he ordered, "Let me see that arm."

Lenny held out her injured arm. Gramps winced, red brows bristling. "If that's all you got," he growled, "you're damned lucky. Takes a dumb city gal to tangle with a bobcat!"

Above Soapy's excited racket, Lenny protested, "But she took Ringo. She had him in her mouth."

"The kitten?"

Lenny nodded. "It wasn't a bobcat," she persisted. "It was just a big tabby."

"Some tabby," Gramps grunted sourly, peering at her arm.

"Ever see a house cat with claws set *that* far apart?"

By the time they reached the farmhouse, Gramps had worked himself into a typical "Sid Bloom temper." "Sheddap!" he yelled at Soapy. "We all know the cat was there." And pointing his pipe at Lenny, he added, "So did she. Told her so just last night. 'Stay out of the orchard,' I said."

"Lots of people mistake bobcats for house cats," Todd put in.

Gramps thrust his face into Lenny's. "That cat had tufts on its ears, didn't it?" he demanded. "And a short tail?"

"I don't. . ." Lenny started, then lapsed into silence. Her arm throbbed painfully and the sky, beginning to wheel, had dark patches blotting the blue. "I'm going to faint," she groaned. The veranda steps heaved unnaturally, but with Todd's hand beneath her elbow she managed to climb them. Then a too-dim kitchen and something to sit on, Gram's concerned exclamation, and the sharp cold sting of antiseptic.

Gramps's cracked old voice rasped on and on. Maybe I am all the things he says: feather-brain, addlepate, and dimple dome. But there's a thing called good manners, Lenny thought angrily. Apparently Sid Bloom had never heard of manners.

"Damn you!" she said coldly. Suddenly the kitchen cleared, the sun streaming through the curtains and catching the glint of laughter in Todd's eyes. Gram wore a disapproving look and Gramps a slack-mouthed stare. "Thanks!" he snorted and stamped out of the house.

"I'm sorry," Lenny murmured, not really meaning it.

"He deserved it," was Gram's surprising reply. "Sid always blows off steam when he's upset."

Todd changed the subject. "Shouldn't Lenny see a doctor? I could take her into town in the cruiser."

Lenny laughed. "For a cat scratch?"

His face was serious. "Not funny," he retorted. "That cat might've been rabid."

Gram's hand flew to her mouth. "Good heavens!"

"Don't be silly," Lenny said. "You're frightening Gram." Me too, she thought, trying to ignore the definite stiffening of her fingers and the puffy stretched look of her hand.

"It was a beautiful creature," she chattered brightly. "Like a big Persian. I'm sure it wouldn't have touched me if I hadn't sneaked up on it."

"It was a bobcat," Todd told her firmly, "with a ruff and tufted ears. Tomorrow, Mr. Bloom and I are going to trail it. See if we can gun it down."

Lenny stared. "You wouldn't! Bobcats hardly ever bother people. So why kill it? Besides," she argued, "she has Ringo. Why would a bobcat carry off a house kitten?" Through the screen door, Gramps supplied the answer. "For lunch," he said. "What else?"

Lenny swung on him. "Gramps!"

"Now, now," Gram interceded. "Stop it, you two." To Lenny, she ordered, "Up the stairs, young lady, and change that soiled top. Then Todd will take you to the doctor."

In the bedroom, Lenny struggled with her jersey and a returning wave of nausea. Abruptly she sat on the bed, imagining a helpless Ringo being torn apart, screaming with pain and dying horribly. If I don't stop this, she told herself, I'm going to bring up.

It probably was a bobcat, though, she conceded, recalling her glimpse of the cat as it whirled away — the gray-brown underbelly and the decided fullness, not all of it fur. Gramps is just being deliberately mean. The cat wouldn't kill Ringo! She had carried the kitten by the scruff of the neck, the way every mother cat did. Maybe she had just lost her own litter and needed a kitten to nurse. Nobody's going to hunt you down, she promised fiercely, tugging at a white tank top.

It was a crazy kind of promise, she knew. But with it, the sick feeling disappeared and she managed, despite a very tender arm, to straighten the bed covers, run a comb through her hair and answer a pleasant, "Coming," to Gram's now familiar reminder that Todd was waiting. He's been waiting all morning, was Lenny's happy thought.

"How are you going into town?" Gramps asked.

"I'll take *The Scotsman*," Todd replied. "If nobody's using her."

He turned to Lenny as she came down the stairs. "Feel like walking to Ipperwash? Or shall I bring the boat into the bay?"

Gramps sputtered. "You crazy, son? Over the sandbar? She'll scrape bottom."

"I don't think so, sir. The water's high this year."

Whether it was the "sir" or Gramp's obvious liking for Todd, Lenny didn't know. But there was a hint of camaraderie in the older man's reply. "Try anythin', won't you, son?"

Todd grinned. "Just about, sir," he said. "Anything I think I can manage." His eyes challenged Lenny's. "What'll it be, Miss O'Hare? A walk through the woods? Or, a pick-up at the dock?"

"I've already been picked up at the dock," she retorted. "Let's try the woods."

The woods, too, were different. The walk seemed much shorter than it had been five years ago; the path was well beaten and swept clean of its carpet of needles. But there was still the pungent perfume of pine and the charm of pink and white twinflowers dotting the edge of the path. And the ruby sparkle of wild strawberries had not changed.

Ahead of Lenny, Todd deposited his eggs on the path and stooped to pick berries. Popping one into his mouth, he turned to dangle another under her nose. Without thought, she opened her mouth to receive it.

"Uh - uh," he said, smiling. "No goodies for Lenny — till Todd gets his." He was holding the fruit out of reach and slowly shaking his head. He was also standing very close; she could see the blond fuzz on his jaw, the yellow flecks in his eyes.

Heart pounding and sure that Todd could see it, Lenny was a battleground of "do's" and "don'ts." If I don't he'll think I'm a creep. If I do, he'll think I'm a pushover. Her arms shot out, palms smacking against his chest, and the thud brought a gasp of pain. With the pain, came Mom's voice almost as if she stood at Lenny's elbow. "Never be too easy, dear. That kind of news really travels."

"You can tell your friend in the black trunks," Lenny said coldly, "that you've lost your bet."

Todd had the grace to flush. Knowing that she'd guessed correctly, Lenny swung about and headed back to the farm. With every step, the hard lump in her chest grew larger. I *wanted* him to kiss me, she thought. But not for a bet! Not that way!

"Hey!" he called after her. "I thought we had a doctor's appointment."

Still trudging in the opposite direction and not looking back, she asked, "What appointment? Nobody made one."

"Don't be dumb. That arm needs attention. Besides, the 'doc' is my uncle. So no sweat. We won't need an appointment."

"I'll bet," she cried over her shoulder. "You can fix just about everything, can't you?" You and your rich parents, she wanted to add. Your plushy summer home and your big boats!

Angry at Todd, and at herself for being so childish, Lenny realized she was wrecking her first real chance at a "fun" summer. What does a bet matter, she asked herself. Mom doesn't know what she's talking about; wanting me to be a square, to be left out of everything that matters. I'll have nothing but my self respect. And what good is that?

Rounding the bend in the path, her steps slowed. This time, she felt sure Todd wouldn't follow. I'll wait, though, she decided. If he doesn't come, I'll go back and say something clever like, "Joke over."

Picking silvered flakes from a giant uprooted tree at the path's edge, she stood quietly and waited.

6 A Hex Day

The upended tree with its huge roots exposed seemed vaguely familiar. But the faint memory was unimportant compared with the immediacy of the moment. I'll count to ten, Lenny thought. Ten slivers of bark. Then I'll go back to Todd.

"*One, two . . .*" A flirt of yellow wings flashed in some low-growing scrub oak. Wild canary, she thought, or maybe a goldfinch. "*Three, four. . .*" If he's coming, I won't hear him; he's not wearing shoes. Up there was the barest suggestion of a trail. Leading where? "*Five, six. . .*" No sound, only the throaty bagpiping of a hidden tree toad. Todd is listening too, she concluded exultantly. I can feel it.

At the count of eight, his voice broke the stillness. "Hi," he said. But his greeting was not intended for Lenny, nor did it sound as if he'd moved from the spot where she'd left him.

"What gives?" Black Trunks was asking.

"What's it look like?" Todd asked him, flippantly. "Hatching eggs."

There was a short, puzzled silence. Then Black Trunks's triumphant hoot. "Brush-off!" he shouted. "Lover-boy finally got the brush-off."

"Stow it, Mann."

"Barney's the name. Barney Mann."

"Same difference," Todd retorted.

They were moving off in the direction of Ipperwash, their voices fading. But Lenny's straining ears caught Black Trunks's reminder that Todd owed him a fiver. And something about the girls waiting to water-ski. Then Todd — it couldn't be Todd!

"Dumb broad," he said.

The remark hurt worse than Lenny's arm, throbbing in her throat and smarting her eyes. I hate that word. Hate it! That was the end, the absolute end — Mr. Todd Brewster could stay where he belonged. And so would Lenny O'Hare. He in his pink summer residence; she in a little wooden farmhouse.

Her feet, of their own volition, turned off the main path. She skirted the sprawled length of a dead tree, avoided the knotty toughness of scrub oak and entered the bush. Dense sumac reared up ahead, but she pushed it aside knowing the path was still there, feeling its beaten presence through the thin soles of her runners.

The sun, now directly overhead, sent hot ribboned light through a stand of slender white birch. At the meadow's edge, tiny ghost-curls steamed mistily at the cool feet of ancient fir, their trunks close-packed and bare, their crowns reaching high and jostling the sky.

Not yet aware of the heat, Lenny still burned inwardly with resentment. What does Todd think he's doing? Slumming? Todd's whole morning build-up had led to only one end: a pass in the woods. I was just for "kicks", she concluded glumly.

"Oh rats!" she said aloud, her angry voice a small lost sound under the thick arch of green. With it came the certain knowledge that she had been there before; there had been a path and a little-girl secret. And steps leading to nowhere.

How old had she been? Eight, maybe? Stumbling upon the path purely by accident, she had followed it in ever-increasing enchantment. Then, its width had been large enough for a child. Now, placing one foot blindly in front of the other, she fought for balance in the narrow leaf-lined tunnel.

Obviously, no human had travelled here for quite some time. But there had been animals; there in a sundappled spot of moist earth were paw marks raking backward and leaving small mounds of leaves. A dog, Lenny surmised. Soapy could've stopped for a moment to scratch and then charge on. Later, Lenny would try to recall if there were any claw marks between the four-inch ridges of dirt. Or were they made by cat pads with claws deliberately sheathed?

But now, her only thought was to push on, away from the hurt of Todd; away from the Blooms and their funny little farm; away from her mother and father and the endless bickering. She just wanted to be alone. If only she had a *home* to go back to!

Tears streaked Lenny's face when she stepped into the glade. After five years, it was unchanged: a natural circle of columned trunks, their branches curved like the fingers of two hands meeting tip to tip. It reminded Lenny of a place of worship: sunlight arrowing down and filling the place with soft radiance.

In the circle's centre was the great rock. Flat-topped, with steps leading upward, it could have been an altar with its whole surface draped in the green velvet of lichen and moss.

Surprisingly, the four steps were not of Nature's doing. Nature, though, had done her best to make it seem so, smoothing the bricks with wind and rain, softening the mortar between, and extending her broadloom of moss from top to bottom.

Why, Lenny wondered afresh, would anyone want to build steps in the middle of a forest? There were no tree stumps to indicate a widening of the glade, no beginnings of a foundation for cottage or for cabin. Only the steps — and the flat expanse of rock. Whatever the reason, she was glad of this lovely, untouched place, glad because she was here alone in the quiet. Soundlessly, her feet ascended the steps. Going nowhere, she thought, with nothing to do but sit cross-legged on a mossy cushion — not to think, not to worry, not to get hurt.

High above, a song sparrow whistled three sweet notes followed by a tiny explosion of melody. Leaning back in an effort to spot the songster, Lenny straightened with a gasp, her injured arm pulsing with pain. Decidedly right-handed, she'd had no cause to use the left one, had felt no actual discomfort. But now, jarring waves travelled from shoulder to wrist and with the pain came the awareness that she was indeed acting foolishly.

Rising to her feet, Lenny stood a moment, reluctant to leave the magic of this place which seemed solely her own. But she would come back; it would always be here. She noted that the path went on, the same adventurous animal having left a trail of scratch marks in his wake. Tomorrow she would follow it, see where it led. At least it would be a start in her search for Ringo.

Today, she would have to retrace her steps, face the Blooms, and confess to not seeing the doctor. And tell them... what? That Todd had made a pass at her? That she'd run off...?

But there was no need to invent a story. The weather provided a convenient one for her; great cumulus clouds were piling rapidly overhead. By the time Lenny reached the farmhouse, thunderheads blotted out the sun and ragged gusts of wind were lashing waves far out in the lake.

Gram was waiting on the veranda as Lenny and Gramps dashed for shelter, heavy drops of rain dotting their path, the treetops quivering under the sudden downpour.

Shaking his wet helmet and rubbing it dry on his sleeve, Gramps remarked, "Sensible kid, Todd. Wise not to try for town in this weather."

But Gram was anxious. "What about Lenny's arm?"

Grateful to the storm for relieving her of an explanation, Lenny was optimistic. "The arm's fine," she said. "It can wait till tomorrow."

"I'll take her in to the doctor's," Gramps offered. "This weather'll blow over fast."

Lenny's heart sank. Oh, no! Not in the *Pixie*! I couldn't take another crazy situation.

But Gram voiced the same opinion. "Not in the *Pixie*, you won't. I'll take her in my boat."

"You have another boat?" This whole day was beginning to take on a science-fiction quality, Lenny thought.

In the old-fashioned kitchen, she helped Gram set a late lunch table with crockery Lenny knew to be dime-store quality. Yet here was Gram informing her that they owned a new twin-prow, 75 horsepower motorboat.

"Sid's fond of the *Pixie*," Gram explained. "But," she added with a twinkle, "it's one thing to be fond of that boat. And another to ride in her! You'll like the *Sea Nymph*."

Gramps's weather prediction proved correct; the storm blew itself out within the hour and the sun shone brightly again. And "liking" the *Sea Nymph* was an understatement; Lenny enjoyed every moment of her trip into town. The craft was completely modern, a blaze of streamlined scarlet as she streaked into Rock's End leaving every other boater behind.

In the doctor's waiting room, Lenny kept trying to curb a bubble of laughter at mental pictures of Gram standing at the wheel as the *Sea Nymph* passed other craft without effort, her hand raised in nonchalant salute.

The return trip, though, was not as funny. The doctor's poking, the cleansing and the needle all added up to a very tender arm. Today, Lenny decided fuzzily, was certainly a "hex" day. As they sped homeward, the ominous devil's face painted on a rock at the opening of Satan's Gorge seemed to confirm her feelings.

That evening, her offer to help with the dinner dishes received a firm rejection from Gram. "You sit with your feet up in the parlour," she said, "and keep Sid company."

As it turned out, Gramps did the entertaining. His stories about Rock's End's early days were always worth listening to. "Know how Satan's Gorge got its name?" he demanded.

Lenny shook her head; she had always thought it was because of the horrible face painted on the rock at the opening of the channel.

"Nope," Gramps said. "The Indians didn't paint that rock. The whites did. Nowadays, the fellows who're commissioned by the government to paint the buoys usually finish up painting the rock. It's gotten to be sort of custom."

His voice droned on and, to keep awake, Lenny counted the blue Copenhagen plates on Gram's wall, the roses in one section of the wallpaper — anything rather than insult Gramps twice in one day.

At any other time, his story would have kept her

entranced: the two Indian war canoes of opposing tribes and their unexpected meeting at the narrow channel-opening. She could almost see the flashing blades, the locked canoes, the brief but fierce struggle. Then both craft, with all warriors, were sucked beneath the surface in the deadly whirlpool. "That's one reason for the name Satan's Gorge," he said.

"There's a kind of religion about the rocks as well," he went on. "That painted one in particular. Even today, you'll see little offerings at its base. Fish, berries and corn to ensure good crops and plentiful fishing."

Lenny shivered, thinking about Satan's Gorge. It was creepy, the black circling roll of the water, the towering rocks on either side — and the horrible face leering down.

She jumped when Gram, standing at the chairback, put a hand, still damp from dishwater, on her forehead. "You, young lady, have a chill," she announced. "Up to bed you go!"

Making no objection, Lenny climbed the stairs obediently, wishing she could crawl under the sheets without the bother of undressing, or even of cleaning her teeth.

Gram's goose-down pillows felt good beneath her head; the fresh sheets smelled of cedar and lavender. Through heavy lids, she could see the sunset: Indian red misted with yellow. A long time since I've gone to bed with the sun, was her rueful thought. A real "fun" summer!

I meet a boy and manage to lose him in one short day. Gramps gives me a kitten — and it gets carried off. Todd I might have to forget, but Ringo I'm going to find!

7 "A Creature of the Night"

Rain slapped fitfully at the window when Lenny wakened. Or was it wet birch fringes brushing the pane? Whatever it was, she thought, the day offered nothing worth the effort of getting up. Turning over, she pressed her cheek into the pillow, the movement reminding her that she still nursed a sore arm. There was also a strange tightness about her face, a swollen feeling. Touching it, she came fully awake, swinging her legs free of covers and heading for the dresser.

"Bro - ther!" she exclaimed to her reflection. Her face was not her own, lips pushed into a baby-pout by too-fat cheeks and heavy lids making blue slits of eyes only half their usual size. Even her fingers resembled plump sausages!

The penicillin, of course! She'd forgotten to warn the doctor about her usual reaction. That does it, she thought tearfully. I *am* hexed. Who else but Lenny O'Hare could have so many things go wrong?

She was still sitting on the dresser bench when Gramps appeared at the door with a breakfast tray.

"Good morn. . ." he began, his expression changing so comically that Lenny would have laughed — if she'd been able.

"Holy Toledo!" he said, thumping down the tray. A second look at Lenny's face and he was dashing to the head of the stairs, shouting, "Laura! Come up here!"

Lenny could have told them what the doctor would say. Gram came from a hurried phone call with instructions to "stay in bed and no milk, no condiments, no chocolate, soft drinks, *et cetera*."

45

"If it gets worse, I'm to let him know," she added.

From the kitchen, Gramps's remark came clearly up the stair well. "That's a relief," he chuckled. "I thought for a minute I'd done a Rip Van Winkle. Slept through the summer and woke up on Hallowe'en.

"Now, Sid, that's enough. Lenny will hear you."

"So what? Nowadays kids have no sense of humour. Don't know how to laugh at themselves."

Lenny snorted. "I'd like to see *him* laugh when he's blown up like a balloon."

But Gramps's face held no hint of laughter when he came to collect Lenny's breakfast tray. "No appetite, huh?" he said, surveying her untouched plate. The buckwheat pancakes were Lenny's favourite and Gram had fried them to a crisp brown. Even the jug brimming with maple syrup had been uninviting; the only thing she'd been able to get down was a grapefruit half.

"I'm sorry," Lenny said, half expecting Gramps's usual harangue on the waste of good food.

" 'S okay," he grunted unexpectedly. "We'll save 'em for tomorrow." Pulling a folded magazine from his overalls' pocket, he held it out. "Brought this up. Has an article on bobcats. Thought you might be interested."

Lenny shot him a quick glance, searching his face for sarcasm. After yesterday and all the insulting remarks about dumb "city gals," she suspected this was just another excuse to prove his point. But his faded blue eyes held only sympathy, the proffered book only a kindly thought.

Taking the well-thumbed *National Geographic*, Lenny tried to stretch her swollen lips into a grateful smile. "Thanks," she said. "If I'm going to rescue Ringo, I'll need to know all about bobcats."

The moment the words were out, she knew they were a mistake. Gramps's smile disappeared, his eyes hardened and his mouth became a thin, tight line. "You got rocks in your head, girl?" he demanded. "You can't rescue any kitten. Not from a bobcat, you can't."

He jabbed a finger at the book in Lenny's lap. "Read that," he ordered. "Then, you'll see why."

Leaning back on the pillows, Lenny heard the clump of his feet on the stairs and the clank of a metal tray on the kitchen sideboard. "That girl," he announced loudly, "is an idiot!"

"Mind your manners, Sid," Gram shot back. "Lenny's a lovely girl — and you know it. At the moment, she's upset. Also," she added slowly, "I have a feeling that finding Ringo is very important."

"Women!" Gramps exploded. "And their feelings! Well, she isn't gonna track no bobcat. Not while she's under my care. You want her to get herself mauled again?"

The screen door slammed, followed by the sucking sound of heavy boots on the muddy path. Lenny sighed. I guess I am an idiot, she conceded bleakly. No wonder I can't make friends. Everything I do is wrong. Gram is the only one who likes me. Even Mom and Dad have gone off without me.

Thunder rumbled on the far side of the lake. A rotten, stinking day, she thought, turning the pages without interest. She paused at a full-page photo of a cat. Probably Gramps's bobcat.

Glaring at Lenny with black ringed eyes, its heavily furred face was split with hate: lips drawn back, whiskers curved down, and hair-tipped ears level with its head. The animal was contorted with fury. Whatever danger it faced, she thought, there was not one hint of fear. Ready to fight rather than run, it would destroy everything in its path — including itself if necessary!

"A creature of the night," the first sentence began, "the bobcat prowls on velvet paws. . . ." Twenty pages in length, the article was really an excerpt from a forthcoming book. Lenny was still reading, when downstairs a girl's voice called, "Mrs. Bloom? Are you in?"

"Debra," Gram welcomed her. "Debra Brewster. How nice to see you." Then, "Surely, you can't need more eggs. Only yesterday, Todd took four dozen."

At the mention of Todd's name, Lenny lowered the book,

listening. Debra, whoever she was, had a pretty laugh.

"Not for a week or so," she said. "There'll be a crowd, though, later on. Some of them will be staying for my birthday."

"Oh, my. I forgot about the big party. I'll have to keep some of the eggs for your angel cake. Does your mother have some help? Is Mrs. Ragout still housekeeping?"

"Rags? Oh, yes. We Brewsters couldn't exist without Rags."

So Debra is Todd's sister, Lenny thought.

Gramps joined them in the kitchen. "You folks still celebrating with the usual bonfire?" he asked.

"That!" Debra exclaimed. "I wish they wouldn't. It's silly."

"You may get your wish," Gramps told her. "With so little rain this summer, you may not get a licence for a fire that big."

"Suits me," the girl replied. "It isn't really my celebration anymore, anyway. It's the older folks'." Her laugh tinkled up the stairs. "For years, we kids had our own little party; then we were stuck in bed while our parents had a ball."

"Well," Gram remarked. "Not many people get themselves born at a summer cottage. Round here, your fire is sort of tradition."

Debra sounded dubious. "I suppose so," she said.

Lenny shifted her position. The pillows sagged lumpily at her back and the movement started the magazine's pages turning of their own accord. A bobcat grimaced up at her with a toothy, four-pronged smile. "Aarr--gh, yourself," she said, aloud, and poked a finger at the cat's paper nose.

She must have missed some of the downstairs conversation because Gram was halfway up to the bedroom. "I'll see if she's awake," she was saying. "I'm sure Lenny would love to meet you."

I would not! Lenny thought indignantly. Not looking like this! Her quick pretense of sleep, the sheet drawn partly over her face, was apparently good enough for Gram. Coming into the room, she stayed only a moment, then left quietly.

"Asleep," she announced. "I'll pass along your invitation to the party."

"It's really Todd's invitation," Debra said. "For some reason he wanted me to ask Lenny. Don't ask me why."

"Maybe he's shy," Gram supplied helpfully.

Under the sheets, Lenny snorted, "Shy!" She hadn't meant to say it aloud, but Debra's laugh covered the sound.

"Todd, shy!" she said, her sarcasm easy to detect.

When Debra left, curiosity carried Lenny to the window. Obscured by the curtains and a hanging frond of birch, she watched till the girl reached the gate, stopping to unlatch it. She's not in the least like Todd, Lenny thought with surprise. Tiny, barely topping the picket fence, Debra was almost witch-skinny and had dark hair swinging below her shoulder blades.

I'd like to get to know her, Lenny decided. No particular reason; just that Debra seemed to have no illusions about Todd. So what does that mean? Lenny asked herself. It means, she concluded honestly, that I *did* have illusions — and they got mangled! Just because Todd looks such a dream, I expected him to act like one. Well, I'm not accepting any second-hand invitation. He can ask me to the party himself!

Leafing through the magazine in bed, Lenny was well aware that her chances of receiving Todd's personal invitation were very slim indeed. But in spite of everything that had happened, she admitted to hoping that she might see Todd Brewster again.

For the next two days, Gram remained adamant about Lenny's staying in bed. "You're to stay put," she said. "Until every smitch of that swelling disappears. That's what the doctor said."

The weather continued cloudy and cool and Lenny's allergy took its time about disappearing. So there was nothing to do but read *National Geographic*s and yearn for a letter from Mom and Dad. If only I knew where they were, she thought. Or where they were going to settle for a day or two. Then I could send a letter ahead.

Why couldn't she have parents like other girls? A father with a steady job and a salary. A house where they would stay longer than a year. Why didn't her Dad realize how embarrassing it was to have people at the door wanting to be paid?

Lenny could sympathize with her mother, but she didn't love Dad any less. Her most frightening thought was that maybe her mother had changed. Why else would she speak the way she had that last day before Lenny left for the lake.

"Writing is your chosen profession and I understand the difficulties," she had said. "But face it, Shaun. You can't support a family. And I won't live any longer on credit. How do you expect me even to dress your daughter — with no money for material?"

"You'll get your money. I've been given the go-ahead on my last query."

"Oh Shaun! Give it up and get a job. With your writing experience, you could. You *know* you could."

"So we're back to that. A nice tidy office and a steady income."

"I thought marriage was a fifty-fifty affair. Ours seems to be lopsided. Or haven't you noticed? I'm tired, Shaun, working for fifteen years to supplement your failures.

"Thanks!"

"Shaun, I just can't take it anymore. If this trip to the States doesn't work, I'll have to make my own plans."

Her voice had been cold as if all the arguments through the years had condensed into this last, frozen ultimatum.

Later that night Lenny had missed Mittens on the bed. Alternately she had hated her parents — and loved them: not wanting to be with them, yet hurt because they preferred to take this trip without her. Finally she had fallen asleep with her head buried under the quilt — to muffle the sound of her tears.

In an effort to blot out the memory, Lenny concentrated on the bobcat article, memorizing it almost word for word. I don't care what Gramps says, she thought defiantly, I'm going to find Ringo and bring him back! It won't be that dangerous.

According to the article, bobcats would not attack unless cornered. There was, of course, the rare cat who'd tasted blood and went on a killing spree. But those were the ones whose regular diet of rodents and birds had been scarce.

Sometimes, too, male bobcats would mate with barn cats. So why wouldn't it be possible for a female to carry off a barn kitten? Expecially, if her kittens had just died. To Lenny, her own thinking made sense.

Somehow, she would track that cat down — the moment the weather cleared and Gram allowed her out of bed.

8 On the Trail

On Sunday, the sun burnt through the last remnants of cloud, polishing each leaf on every tree and colouring afresh a rain-clean world.

Church bells chimed from town, fanning over the lake and repeating themselves in echoed reminders. From the front porch Lenny waved goodbye to Gram and Gramps, and at the gate, Gramps lifted his hymn book in final salute. He looked unfamiliar and slightly uncomfortable in a dark suit and starched white shirt. "Some excuse!" he called back with a grin.

"Take care, Lenny," Gram added. "It's your first day out of bed."

She's pretty, Lenny thought, for an old lady. Gram's navy suit hung smartly on her sparse little body and a pink flowered hat softened the severity of her hair.

Lenny nodded emphatically, excusing herself on the grounds that if she didn't say anything, it might not be such a lie. She had no intention of "taking care" of herself. She intended waiting only till the *Sea Nymph*'s motor faded into the distance. Then, she had about two hours to start trailing a bobcat.

During the fifteen minutes it took Gram and Gramps to reach the boathouse and the resulting roar of the *Sea Nymph*'s departure, Lenny busied herself making a sandwich and getting dressed. She threw on black jeans and a dark shirt hoping to blend inconspicuously with the forest growth.

Having sprayed herself liberally with insect repellent, she started off. Another ten minutes was lost when Soapy insisted on accompanying her and was consequently locked in the barn. Lenny hated to do it; she could hear his woeful moaning and the scratch of his claws on the door. By the time he found the other opening at the back, she hoped to be far enough away to discourage any pursuit. Soapy's noisy company was out of the question. He would simply alert every animal for miles.

It was good to be outdoors again. The path leading to Ipperwash was bright with morning sun and song sparrows filled the air with joyous whistles. The upturned tree roots pointed silver-grey fingers to the hidden path and Lenny hesitated only long enough to make sure she went unseen. Then she sprinted the short distance to the concealing trees.

After three days of steady rain, every growing thing was spangled with moisture, and the path was soggy beneath her feet. Even the glade, breathtakingly beautiful in its morning freshness, was too wet for comfort. The rock, a brilliant green sponge, oozed water at the slight touch of her hand.

Lingering a moment, Lenny wondered what it was the glade possessed. Other than beauty there was an indescribable something, a something that erased all fear. Maybe, she thought, because all ugliness was sealed off. As if serenity and peace of mind had been crystallized into one small pocket.

She was at that moment intensely aware of her own youth, the long clean line of waist and thigh, the swelling curve of breast, the silky swing of hair brushing her cheek. She did not attempt to analyse her feelings, she simply enjoyed them. She knew only that she was, indeed, a part of the glade; that she belonged.

On the far side of the clearing, the path which Lenny had noted previously was still there. But the paw marks had been washed away. She had hoped to observe them more closely. In the magazine there had been a paragraph given wholly to the way the animal marked its own territory. Apparently, you could tell easily whether it was dog or not. The claw marks of dogs were distinct when raked backward. But bobcats kept their claws sheathed. The males did it deliberately and each mark was the width of a hind foot, two inches or less. There would be a ridge of dirt, the article had said, with leaves or pine needles left between the markings. And it would point in the direction the bobcat was travelling.

The male bobcat made the marks to stake out his own territory and to leave a trail for his mate. And the female, knowing he'd be back, usually stayed somewhere near.

Lenny chuckled. Not a bad idea, she thought, and wondered why humans had changed the system. With the men expected to do all the running!

The path leading out of the glade seemed even smaller than the one leading in. Scarcely a foot in width and choked with growth, it meant pushing one's way through a veritable rain forest. After a few yards, Lenny was drenched. With all this wetness, it would be impossible to tell whether a bobcat had urinated on his markings or not. A fine way to tell your "girl friend" where you were!

Steadily the ground rose and rocks, slippery with moss, began appearing on the path. In the shelter of one, Lenny found her first "marker."

Down on her knees, tape measure in hand, she tried to remember everything she had read. Maybe, just maybe, she was on the right track. The female who'd run off with Ringo might just be following the regular trail of her mate.

According to her watch, Lenny had been climbing for twenty minutes — clambering over windfalls and pulling herself upward by hanging branches. Once she hesitated warily at a huge fallen fir, its hollow stump overgrown with vines. A place like this, the magazine had said, was ideal for a bobcat with kittens. There were instances when a mother cat, surprised by an innocent intruder, had boiled out of her hiding place. Lenny's arm, still tender, was enough reminder for reluctance about tangling twice with a bobcat!

The day promised to be hot. Already the woods were humid and close. Lenny's face beaded with perspiration and her hair hung limply. Breathing heavily, she wished that she'd brought along a thermos of Gram's cold lemonade instead of a sandwich.

Up ahead was a flat, shale-like shelf and somewhere beyond

the tinkling sound of falling water. It looked like a pleasant resting place. Past the shelf the ground levelled off. Although heavily treed, it was, at least, not uphill.

Seated on the shelf and swinging her legs, Lenny took a deep breath of woodland air. Beneath the heavy scent of pine were all sorts of nose-tickling perfumes. At her side, wild honeysuckle bloomed, and picking some, she noticed the curious leaf arrangement behind the flower. Not far away was a dogwood dotted with white berries. And nearby, a plant ran its stems along damp soil in a profusion of tiny, delicate flowers.

She leaned over to look more closely and became suddenly aware of an unpleasant odour. It could be what Gramps called bedstraw; he'd handed her a small bouquet one day and waited with wicked delight while she sniffed.

But this odour was worse than any bedstraw. Scrambling to her feet, Lenny kicked aside a small mound of debris. Beneath the mound was a dead squirrel, half-eaten and crawling with maggots. Lenny's nose wrinkled; then she smiled with triumph. She had unearthed another clue! Bobcats, if they couldn't eat their kill, sometimes covered it up, returning to feed on it later.

The temptation to go charging along the trail was overwhelming. But she managed to curb it. The bobcat's hearing was uncannily keen, aided by tufted hairs on each ear, like antennae.

She had taken only a few steps when she caught the sound of voices coming from flatter ground directly above. Crouching on the slope beside a small pine, Lenny waited as the voices grew louder. Barney Mann and Debra Brewster strolled into sight.

Lenny suddenly realized where she must be: just below the path leading from the Blooms' boathouse. The path from Ipperwash and the boathouse trail must converge at the farm. All she had managed to do was complete the third line of a triangle!

Barney and Debra were having an argument, Debra pointing a rigid finger at the rifle under his arm.

"You can't use that," she protested. "Not here. Not in a populated area."

"Who says?" Barney asked.

"The forest rangers — that's who!" she retorted. "If you're caught, you'll get a stiff fine. And your gun confiscated."

"Who's to catch me?"

Debra shrugged. "It's your funeral," she said.

"You mean a bobcat's funeral," Barney corrected.

He threw his free arm about Debra's shoulder, looking down with a smile. "Aw, c'mon doll. Don't be a party pooper."

For a second, he seemed to be looking directly at Lenny. She held her breath, expelling it slowly as Debra leaned against him, hair shining blackly on his scarlet jersey.

"Nut," she said affectionately. "I don't know why you send me."

Neither did Lenny. Barney Mann stood for so many things that she didn't like: snobbery, rudeness, no respect for rules or for people — not to mention his "bet" with Todd. She had to admit, though, that upon closer inspection he did have a certain kind of dark good looks.

Unexpectedly, Barney made a half-serious, half-joking retort. Removing his arm from Debra's waist and walking apart, he said, "You like losers, maybe?" Debra fielded the question neatly. "You'll lose all right. Most of your allowance if you're fined."

Not till they were past, did Lenny digest the meaning of their conversation and Barney's last remark: "I'll be doing everybody a favour. Already, the cat's mauled the Bloom babe, and killed their dog."

Lenny simmered with indignation. Barney Mann was ruining all her plans. His stupid bet had messed up her friendship with Todd; and now he was hunting the same cat! If he found the bobcat, he might scare her off. Or even worse, he might kill her, leaving Ringo to starve in the woods.

Lenny's watch pointed to half past twelve indicating the imminent arrival of Gram and Gramps. She had intended to put on the kettle and have some lunch ready. The quickest way back to the farm would be the path directly ahead. But the possibility of meeting Barney and Debra was too great. They would question

Lenny's appearance, and she wouldn't blame them. Dirt-crusted hands wiped on damp jeans had left long smears of mud, and her runners had grown in size with at least an inch of the path still sticking to the soles.

Besides, Lenny admitted, I want to make a good first impression on Debra Brewster. She was not sure why it was so important to impress Todd's sister. Nor did she probe too deeply into her secret determination to track down a bobcat and to find a lost barn kitten. Lenny was merely sure that what she was doing had assumed tremendous importance.

Backtracking, she found the going easier, the path slanting downhill, familiar landmarks aiding her rapid return. Nevertheless, her breath came in short gasps, and momentarily, she stopped to lean against a tree. Next time, she thought, I'll take the whole morning. Or maybe a day. I'll borrow Gramps's binoculars and I'll be a bird-watcher — a good enough excuse for spending every waking moment in the bush.

Straightening, Lenny felt the pull of tree resin on her shirt. Freeing herself, her eyes travelled upward, marvelling at the tree's height. A beauty, she thought, a perfect specimen of . . . what? Last year, she and four other girls at school had done a project showing the difference between pines, spruce and firs. She wondered if she could identify this one. Too branchy for a mid-continent pine, she decided. So it must be a spruce.

Three fingerlike cones caught her attention. A white spruce, she thought with triumph. Each branch perfectly spaced, it soared skyward in a magnificent spire. A great tree to climb, was her next thought, an ideal lookout.

The first branch was conveniently close to the ground. But the next, much higher, meant remembering how to grip with knees and to dig toes into scaled bark. After that, Lenny's main difficulty was to find space enough to inch through the needle-packed density.

Hands sticky with tree-gum and hair prickled with needles, she stopped two-thirds of the way up. One arm circling the trunk, the other testing a branch for strength, she eased carefully to a sitting position. Then, her breath catching in her throat, Lenny surveyed the picture below: the farm, the lake, and the rocky ridge leading to Satan's Gorge.

A breeze swayed the spruce, filling her nostrils with the richness of crushed needles. Being so high filled her with a wildness, a kind of freedom one didn't experience on the ground. Why? Was it because she was looking down on people? Being in a place no human had a right to be?

The sputter of motorboats at the town dock came clearly on the same breeze. Church must be over, Lenny thought, and prepared to scramble from her perch. But her hair tangled on a branch, making her pause long enough to notice a movement on the high ridge. Head at a stiff angle, one hand loosening a knotted tress, Lenny caught the cat's outline.

Sliding silkily from rock to rock, the animal was perfectly camouflaged against the mottled gray of the ridge. Only its movement and Lenny's precarious position made its discovery possible. She watched while it stood motionless, its head outlined against the sky. Then it disappeared, melting into the landscape as though it had never existed. "But, it *was* there! I *did* see it!" Lenny breathed. She had been on the right trail. The path leading up and over the Blooms' path dipped, then climbed again to the ridge beyond.

Lenny's excitement carried her down the tree, through the glade and back to the farm. From here on, she thought, it should be easy. But how she could conceal her success, or suppress her impatience while she waited for tomorrow, she had no idea.

9 Bobcat Bait

Next morning, Lenny set off surprised that her plans had fallen into place so neatly. Gramps had even suggested that she travel on the "high" path. Handing over his prized binoculars, he'd said, "Just before you hit the rocks is where you'll find birds. Lots of 'em. Take the high path and head toward the ridge."

Lenny accepted both the binoculars and his advice with mixed emotions: guilt at her own deception, delight that her plans were without obstacle. Yesterday, Gram had merely clucked her tongue when she found Lenny's jeans drying on the line. And this morning before sun-up, they had both greeted her at the breakfast table with only obvious pleasure at sharing her company. The latter had been cause for another tremor of guilt and the overwhelming urge to blurt out the whole exciting discovery. That, of course, was out of the question. Gramps's friendly taunts about setting the clock wrong might have changed to instant anger; Gram's happiness about Lenny's active interest in "our little feathered friends" would have been replaced with worried disapproval.

Lenny's misgivings lasted only the time it took to reach the high path. Stopping to catch her breath, adjusting the small knapsack in which Gram had put her lunch, she wished she had time to watch the day's birth. Already a widening rim of lavender sky topped with amber cloud-scarves promised a lovely sunrise. The woods, too, were stirring with a multitude of sounds: birds warming up for their morning symphony and the rustlings and scurryings of small forest life. But night creatures like the bobcat would be settling down for a good day's sleep, Lenny thought. She would have to hurry if she hoped to reach the ridge before sun-up — to catch a glimpse of her quarry.

Sighting yesterday's "lookout" tree and attempting to line up the trail with the one she'd travelled before, Lenny was disappointed to find no obvious continuation of a path. Aware of being etched against the sky from the farm below, she knew her activity could be seen clearly. In the opposite direction, a plume of smoke rising from Ipperwash's fieldstone chimney meant that someone else was also awake. It might even mean that the same someone intended an early plunge off the Brewster pier. Ipperwash was screened by trees, but the floating dock visible from Lenny's vantage point was rising and falling on the lazy morning swell. A person only has to look from there to here, she thought, and I'd be spotted.

As if her mind had conjured up the event, Todd strolled into view. Against the satin-gray of water in the pre-dawn light, his blondness appeared whitely unreal, his scarlet swim-trunks aflame with colour. As he turned to drape his sweatshirt on a piling, it seemed inevitable that Todd should see her. For one heart-stopped second, they were the only two persons in the morning world. Then, arcing into the lake, Todd broke its cool surface in a clean dive. The dreamlike quality of the moment was broken. Lenny breathed a sigh of relief.

Somewhere a bird chuckled and a chipmunk darted through the foxtails. His striped body threaded the tall stalks, swaying their tasselled tops and revealing the hidden path.

Lenny followed it, not looking back, not waiting for Todd's reappearance. Although she was glad he had not seen her, she wished he was at her side. I'm a kook, she thought with annoyance. How can any sane person wish for two distinctly opposite things?

The deeper the path dipped, the more shadowed it became. Thick-growing brush obscured anything underfoot and high-crowned trees made a dense canopy overhead. Leaves slapped wetly at Lenny's face and bad-tempered mosquitoes whined

60

about her ears. She was glad she'd worn a kerchief on her head. Tied turban-fashion, it sprouted two pointed ends from its knot. She wouldn't win any beauty contests, but at least her hair was protected from the spider webs strung stickily across the path.

Once, feet slipping on a mossy knob of rock, she sat heavily on her rump, the impact jarring the breath from her body and whooshing it out in a loud "humm--ff". The noise stilled every sound of forest life. Birds stopped in mid-note and the business of woodland breakfast came to an abrupt halt. Boy! she thought. I sure announced my presence. If I'd blown a bugle, I couldn't have done it better! Even the leaves had quivered to a standstill.

Quietly, Lenny sat where she had fallen. Good sense told her that she was being foolish. Everything she had read, everything she'd been told was against an expedition of this kind. A teenage girl tracking down an animal known, despite its size, to be one of the most vicious! "Licking one's weight in wildcats" had been high compliment for any early-day pioneer. What's so important? she wondered. Besides finding Ringo, why do I want to do this so much?

The question remained unanswered. At Lenny's feet, a bullfrog belched rudely, and water bubbled close by. Accustomed now to the dimness, she realized that two steps further — and she might have been swimming! Then came the knowledge that a stream-bed meant the bottom of the hollow, and possibly rising land on the far bank.

The stream was shallow and easy to cross. But Lenny wasted several minutes splashing about in an effort to find a handhold on the opposite bank. She discovered one, finally, in the form of a tree root, crazily twisted and decidedly slippery. Sneakers slithering along the curves, she lunged out wildly and sprawled heavily onto a bed of wild sweet pea. Getting to her feet, Lenny concluded it was just as well that Todd wasn't here to see. The world's worst woodswoman, she decided. That's me! Todd would laugh himself silly. And she was tired of being laughed at — by Dad, by Gramps and by Todd. Just once she would like someone to listen with real interest to what she had to say, just once to look at her with something other than amusement.

Lenny rose to her feet wearily, then gasped. Long scratch marks on a smooth-barked tree riveted her attention. A cat sharpening its claws? Or getting rid of its cuticle? She didn't know. But there was real satisfaction in the continued discovery of clues.

Self-satisfaction lasted exactly fifteen minutes. Fifteen minutes of steady climbing and a fast-vanishing trail. Chest heaving, Lenny came to a stop in front of a clump of juniper. Close to the ground, it crept in all directions, its crisscross of branches radiating out with no apparent break. If *my* cat went this way, she told herself, she must've bellied underneath.

At Lenny's back, the trees had thinned, their roots grasping feebly at almost non-existent soil, their needles sparse and sickly-looking. Beyond the juniper, rocks began piling up in giant step formation, some spiny or knife-edged, others resembling man-made blocks. Tough weeds bristled between the rocks, defiant tufts growing almost to the ridge-top. Perfect cover for a cat, she decided.

Plunging ahead, Lenny ignored as best she could the sharp pricking of seedling juniper on bare ankles, noting instead that the sun had won the race. Richly yellow, its first rays washed the blunt outcroppings with brilliance, blackening the crevices and inking the caves. Every one of them, she thought, was a possible den site!

Excitement quickened Lenny's step. There was still a chance that the cat had not yet settled for the day. If field mice and rabbits were scarce, the animal might still be on the prowl for some last-minute tidbit. According to the magazine, as long as it was meat, anything would do; bobcats would settle for grasshoppers, beetles, snakes — even lizards.

Overhead, a bird circled and dipped and Lenny reached for Gramps's binoculars. After all, she told herself, I'm supposed to be bird-watching.

For a second, the glasses caught the bird's flight; too far away and too high, its erratic movement made it difficult to pinpoint.

Rock-hopping, climbing from ledge to ledge, Lenny kept the bird in sight. Whatever bothered it was enough to warrant a battle. She could hear its wild chattering as it hovered above one spindly tree which had somehow managed to grow on stone.

A shelf, several yards distant and shadowed partly by overhanging ledge seemed a good vantage point. Heading for it, Lenny suddenly became aware of the height, the dazzle of rising sun and the increasing heat.

The shelf, very narrow and barely large enough to sit on, thinned to a mere twelve inches at either end. Fortunately, her seating space was in shade, and Lenny came to rest with a huge sigh. Then she caught her breath at the view below. I'm on top of the world, she thought. *My* world. A fresh new day full of morning sparkle with nothing to spoil its beauty — except *that*.

"That" was the startling face of Satan's Gorge, leering at Lenny from the rock across the bay. The fanged mouth, the wicked eyes, laughed at her. She shuddered for a moment and wondered if it made everyone feel so uneasy.

The bird, closer now, swooped toward Lenny's perch, almost as if Lenny, herself, was the cause of its distress. It came near enough for her to see the yellow flash of belly, the tiny scarlet splash on its head. A kingbird, perhaps? She'd have to look it up in Gram's bird book. To the tree and back, it swept — to the tree and back.

Obviously, the solitary tree had something to do with the bird's odd behaviour. Training the glasses on it, Lenny instantly spotted the kitten at the base of the trunk.

"Ringo!" she cried. "Its Ringo!" Her reason for quiet forgotten, the shout bounced from rock to rock and echoed in hollow tones. But the damage was done. The kitten was frozen in mid-meal, one paw on his prey, his tiny mouth frilled with feathers. Lenny shuddered. No wonder the mother bird was so frenzied. Her baby was being eaten alive! Already, Ringo had learned the ways of the wild. He'd also grown much bigger and looked quite different; his stripings were darker and his eyes round and fierce.

At that moment, the kitten lifted his head to the rocks above, his black-lined mouth open in what appeared to be a miaow. With the binoculars, Lenny followed the direction of Ringo's call — then gasped. Filling the opening of a small cave was the biggest bobcat she had ever seen. Its head and shoulders took up the whole lens. Horrified, Lenny sat transfixed.

The cat, fat-cheeked with snub nose centred between disc-like eyes, had triangular ears tipped with black. Its sun-yellow stare held no hint of fear, only a stony readiness to deal with Lenny's intrusion. The mouth opened in a wicked, three cornered smile that held an ominous warning. The hissing snarl came very loud — and full of menace.

There was, of course, no need for Gramps's binoculars. The cat, only a few feet distant, stood at a cave opening only slightly higher than Lenny's perch. Lowering the glasses with studied care, she prayed that her movement might not provoke attack.

Already the animal seemed bunched for a leap. Lenny froze, hope for escape plummetting with a sick, sinking sensation. She was forced to face a bitter truth. It had taken five struggling minutes to reach this ledge. Getting down would take longer. *And a bobcat could span the distance in a single leap.*

Down below, someone shot off a rifle, its report popping like a firecracker. The bullet smacked into the rock above. Ears flattened, the cat crouched, then melted into the cave. One moment there; the next, gone.

Lenny, unware that she'd been holding her breath, released it in a soundless whistle. Barney Mann! she thought. Crazy, wonderful Barney! Breaking rules, shooting off guns in populated areas. I love you — love you!

Scrambling on all fours, Lenny began a shaky descent, one leg extended and groping blindly for a lower foothold. The second shot caught her unprepared; hearing the vicious splat, she stared in disbelief at the fresh white wound on the rock's face. Just a foot lower, came the frightening thought, and it might've been me!

"Idiot!" she screamed. "Idiot." But it went unheard. The third shot followed the second with deadly precision. This time, not so close but near enough to flatten Lenny on the ledge, face downward and sobbing. If she stayed, she would be fair game for a bobcat. If she tried to leave, she remained a target for some trigger-happy nut!

Raising her head, Lenny squinted through tears at the cat's cave. It was not there. The kitten, too, had disappeared. At least, there was no movement at the base of the tree. Relief, like warm rain, poured through her body, uncurling her toes, loosening her leg muscles, leaving her limp. But only for a moment. If she could just get off the ledge! Quickly!

Head and shoulders higher now, she scanned the steep drop below. To jump meant landing on jagged rock from a height of at least fifteen feet. Which was better, she wondered fearfully, a broken ankle or a bullet hole?

But the choice was not Lenny's. Another shot cracked in the valley, pinning her to the ledge. Breathing warm rock, tasting gravel, she waited an endless second for the whine, the impact — or worse.

"Mom!" she moaned. "Oh, Mom!"

The sad, hopeless sound brought her to her senses. This time, the bullet had *not* winged her way. There had been no sound indicating a hit. Was it accident? or design?

One dreadful fact remained. Whoever was shooting seemed to be aiming deliberately at Lenny. Her only hope was to remain absolutely motionless — to wait, and to pray.

10 Todd's Confession

How long, Lenny wondered, must she stay on this rocky shelf. Forever? The sun, furnace-hot, and her black clothing sucking up its rays, made each second a torment. Flat on her stomach, Lenny felt her hipbones start to ache as a prickling sensation ran the whole length of her legs. I must move soon, she thought, or I'll be paralyzed. Surely by now, it is safe to move. There had been no more shots and whoever was aiming must have tired of the game.

Lenny's grip on the rock's edge relaxed. At least, my blood's still circulating, she thought with relief. The white scar on the rock was a grisly reminder that it could have been draining from a bullet wound! Why, she asked herself for the hundredth time, would anyone shoot at me? Why, me?

With fear releasing its clutch, she reasoned that the shots were not necessarily meant for her. The gunman, too far away to distinguish anything clearly, might have been popping off at nothing at all. Possibly, just a poor marksman. That was it, she decided. He missed the cat — and nearly got me!

In spite of the heat, Lenny shivered, perspiration turning cool and trickling down her face. What about the second and third shots? Those came *after* the cat had disappeared. The answer, so simple, so logical, had a gruesome kind of humour. *I was the cat!* Wearing dark jeans and blouse, kneeling on all fours, I might easily pass for a cat.

"Oh, Lord!" she whispered hysterically, "I even had ears!" Her black kerchief knotted in two perky ends made a fine substitute for a pair of hair-tipped ears.

It was time to go, but this time, not on all fours. Barely raising her body, Lenny struggled with the kerchief, easing it off and letting it lie where it fell. Now, if her legs would only work, she hoped to shinny, belly-fashion, off the ledge. Surely Barney Mann wouldn't test his marksmanship on a snake! Besides, the shots would most certainly be investigated. By now the Forest Rangers would be hot on his trail. This last thought gave Lenny the needed courage.

Sliding off the ledge, hanging for a moment with trembling fingers, not waiting to gauge a foothold, she dropped. The drop, longer than she had estimated, left her sprawled between two large rocks on a clump of dying juniper. Brittle twigs needling every inch of her back, she lay gasping, and thankful she had missed the sharp outcroppings. A broken leg was the last thing she wanted!

Not till she reached the protective cover of the trees, did Lenny feel the true impact of her experience. Legs suddenly spaghetti, she sank in a heap in the middle of the path. "I could've been killed!" she gasped.

Drinking Gram's lemonade with hands so shaky they chattered the thermos mug against her teeth, Lenny absorbed the blessed quiet of the forest; the near-noon chuckle of birds avoiding the heat, the whisper of water in the stream below. A few moments more, and she'd be ready for the return trip. But not back to the farm; she was not yet prepared to make explanations — or even to tell the truth. The glade, its steps leading nowhere, seemed the natural place to go.

The downhill trail made for easier travelling and the stream was no longer a hazard. Reaching the "high" path, Lenny noted a wisp of smoke rising from Gram's cookhouse. Lunch or dinner seemed to be in progress. But they were not expecting her for lunch, she remembered. She could relax for a while in her favourite place, comb her hair, get rid of twigs and dirt — all the harrowing reminders of a too-recent experience.

But the pleasure of being alone was not to last. Stopping short at the edge of the clearing, she stared at Todd — perched on the moss-draped rock. She had made no attempt at being quiet. In all probability she had sounded like a bull moose thrashing through the brush. But Todd made no sign that he had heard. With his forehead resting on drawn-up knees, he had his arms clasped about his ankles. Lenny's sudden anger at his intrusion could not erase the impression he made. The sun, directly overhead, pencilled the fair curve of his bent head and caught the brown arches of his muscles.

Without raising his head, he said, "So, you're back."

The remark caught Lenny off-balance, mouth open to ask an angry, "What are *you* doing here?" Instead, she snapped, "Back from where?"

His head jerked from his knees and he squinted in the sun. "Oh," he said. "Sorry. I thought you were Barney." Then, eyes adjusting to the light, he grinned. "What happened to you?"

Lenny, suddenly aware of how she looked, pushed a dangling string of hair from her face and brushed ineffectively at her jeans. Then giving it up as hopeless, she glared at him. "Ask your friend, Barney," she replied, voice quivering. "He just finished using me for a target shoot."

Todd straightened up, the look of amusement wiped from his face. "Oh, no!"

"Oh, yes!" Lenny began to shake, her effort to control the tremors only making it worse. "I'm j-just lucky," she gasped, to b-be alive!"

Todd sprang to his feet, hands outstretched and face sober with concern.

"You poor kid. Are you all right."

It was all she needed, sympathy, and someone who cared. "I'm s-sorry!" she sobbed. "But it wasn't funny!"

"I'll bet," he agreed, and led her to the rock, one arm about her heaving shoulders. Seated at her side, he waited quietly for Lenny to regain her composure. "I don't have any Kleenex," he said, finally. "You'll have to use your sleeve."

"I've got some," she said opening her packsack and poking through its contents. Then, dabbing at wet cheeks and blowing her nose, she thought again how nice Todd could be. Without raising her eyes, she remarked, "Every time we meet I seem to be in a flap."

"This time," he told her, "you've got a reason."

She looked up quickly. "And the other times?" Then, staring through wet lashes, she saw Todd's eye, swollen shut and purple-red.

"What happened to *you*?" she exclaimed.

"Same friend," he said. "Barney and I disagreed about a rifle. He wanted to hunt bobcats. I didn't." He touched his eye gingerly, then winced. "Guess I got a little rough trying to convince him."

"Barney's no friend of mine," Lenny announced drily. "Personally, I can't see why he's yours. He's a real creep."

Todd's expression cooled. "My friends happen to be my business. Barney has his own reasons for acting the way he does. Like a few other people I could name."

"Sure!" Lenny retorted. "I've got problems, too. But I don't go around trying to kill people."

"Nothing personal," Todd said, dismissing the subject. "You sure Barney aimed at you?" His voice held disbelief and Lenny sensed his growing dislike for her company. I don't want it that way, she thought suddenly. I want Todd to like me.

"No," she answered, truthfully. "Barney probably thought I was a bobcat."

"A cat!" he exclaimed and threw back his head with a hoot. The sudden movement must have jarred the offending eye and he covered it with his hand, his mouth pursed with pain.

"Serves you right," Lenny observed. "I hope it hurts."

"Thanks."

"You're welcome," she retorted. "If you're so anxious to clear Barney of blame, I'm only trying to help. He couldn't have seen the real bobcat. Because it had already gone back into the cave."

Todd's hand dropped, his good eye puzzled. "Say that again."

Lenny poured out her story: her search for Ringo and how she'd intended to rescue the kitten and bring it home, and the near disaster at the cave. Her voice shook at its finish.

"You know something?" Todd remarked. "You're a dope."

Lenny scrambled to her feet, tugging angrily at the knapsack strap and tumbling Gram's neatly-wrapped lunch onto the rock. Snatching at a wayward apple as it rolled over the edge, she cried, "I shouldn't have told you. I might've known you wouldn't understand!"

Todd caught the apple and held it out. "You're losing your cool again," he observed quietly. Lenny took the apple and scanned his face; he was smiling, but not with amusement.

"Yes," she admitted, slowly. "I guess I am wound up. I suppose," she added, "I'm not very good company."

His smile broadened. "Not very."

Lenny plopped the apple into the sack, closing the flap with a loud snap. "Well!" she said, swinging on her heel. "Good-bye, now!"

"Lenny!" he commanded. "Come back here."

She stopped. "What for?"

"Because," he said, simply, "I want you to."

She hesitated, then retraced her steps. "Bad company and all?"

Todd nodded. "Also," he added mischievously, "I haven't had any lunch."

Lenny smiled. "Neither have I." And taking the knapsack from her shoulder, she set about dividing its contents. "What'll you have? A peanut butter sandwich? Or roast beef?"

Lunch eaten, crumbs, apple cores and paper put tidily away, they lay side by side on the rock. On her stomach, head cradled in her arms, Lenny soaked up the sun, her forehead cool against the moss. Todd lay quietly in the same position. Funny, she thought, I don't mind sharing this place. Todd's being here doesn't spoil it at all; he makes it even better.

Without raising her head, she said drowsily, "I love it here. It's so far away from things."

"Mm—m," Todd said, not moving.

Propping her chin on one arm, she looked at the back of his

head, wanting suddenly to smooth a curl there, to feel the crisp blond hairs change to soft fuzz where it met the nape of his neck.

"You asleep?" she asked, loudly.

"Uh—uh," he said. "Too noisy." He lifted his head. Only inches away, his face contorted unexpectedly. "Wow!" he laughed. "What a pair we are!"

Lenny had not considered her appearance, not for the past half hour. She'd been so at ease in Todd's presence that her tousled hair and dirty face had never entered her mind. "You can say *that* again," she agreed.

Strangely, there was no feeling of embarrassment at Todd's remark. All Lenny knew was that, despite their appearance, she and Todd were enjoying their closeness to each other.

Sitting up, she leaned back straight-armed, face lifted to the sun and eyes closed. Never before had she felt so vibrantly alive. This green-gold place filled her every sense: the soft forest murmur, the summer scent, the leaves, the flowers — her own and Todd's sun-warmed skin.

"At first," she said. "I nearly accused you of being a trespasser."

"You'd be right," Todd replied. "I am."

Lenny's eyes flew open. "How could you know. . . . ." she began.

"Easy. Sid Bloom's got 'No Trespassing' signs tacked to every tree."

"What are you talking about?"

Todd looked perplexed. "Same thing you are, I guess. This here's your granddaddy's property. As if you didn't know."

"You're kidding!"

"You *didn't* know?"

Lenny shook her head. At any other time, in any other place, she might not have said it. But now she confessed.

"Mr. Bloom is really no relation. I just christened him Gramps when I was a kid. I always thought that the Blooms were like my own family." She hesitated. "No money," she ended defiantly.

Todd grinned and held out a hand. "Shake," he said. "Meet

one of the clan."

Too surprised to do anything else, Lenny shook hands. "You?"

Not relinquishing his grasp, Todd swung his legs over the rock's side, and Lenny made no effort to disentangle her fingers.

"Look," he said. "Let's talk."

This, Lenny decided, was not the same Todd. This Todd was the way she had hoped he would be, from the first moment on the Fish Dock.

"To set you straight," Todd began, "my name is not Brewster. It's Todd Adams. I'm Mr. Brewster's stepson — as of one year."

Lenny's mouth opened to ask what difference that made. You still have a rich stepfather, she wanted to say.

"Debra, though," Todd continued, "is a Brewster. And like you, she thinks I'm trespassing."

Lenny interrupted with a laugh. "Oh, Todd. I found this glade when I was ten. And made it mine. That's all. I had no idea that Gramps owned so much land."

"Sid Bloom happens to have owned this whole peninsula at one time," Todd told her. "When he sold the lake front, he must've made a mint."

"I don't believe it."

"It's true."

"I still can't believe it," Lenny said. "That funny old farm. The way Gram and Gramps live."

"Maybe they like it that way."

Lenny detected a trace of bitterness in Todd's voice, and her brows rose.

"Sure," he said. "I like cabin cruisers and my own car. Who wouldn't? So does my mother." He was silent, fingers tightening on Lenny's. She waited, knowing that it was important, knowing that this place, this time, maybe even her own presence could ease Todd's worry.

"It's Debra," he blurted out. "My stepsister's finally gotten through to me. According to Deb, my mother married her father for money. And nothing else."

"So?"

"Well," he replied grimly, "I can't be sure!"

"It could be worse," Lenny reassured him. "Take me, for instance." She had caught his attention. "You *do* have a home," she said. "Even if you're not too comfortable in it."

"What's that supposed to mean?"

"How would you feel," she demanded, "if you couldn't remember any place you could really call home?"

She could see him pondering the question. "You see?" she said.

He nodded. "What's the problem?"

"An Irish father who writes."

Todd's face brightened with interest. Lenny had seen it before; people were always curious about writers. "The problem," she said, flatly, "is that Daddy doesn't sell enough. At least, not enough to support Mom and me."

"So your mother married a struggling writer." His tone told Lenny that he wasn't very impressed.

"Skip it!" she cried. "What's the use!" And snatching her hand from Todd's, she scrambled to her feet.

"Hey! Tell me more." His sharp tug at her blouse brought Lenny abruptly back to his side.

"Cut it out!" she said angrily. "It isn't important."

"Who said?"

Lenny didn't answer. Then the words tumbled out. "Dad's great," she said. "But he's crazy-Irish. To Dad, money doesn't mean a thing. It's just something you hand over to get what you want. If he hasn't got the money, he simply charges it. Then," she added miserably, "you try to dodge the creditors. If you're not good at dodging — you move."

"Where do you live now?" Todd asked.

Lenny looked him square in the eye. "Nowhere," she said. "Dad's dragged my mother to the States. Hunting down assignments, he says. So far, they haven't written to me, so I don't know where they are. Or even if they're still together."

Todd waited, as if he expected more.

73

"That's all," she said. "Except that I don't think my mother can take it much longer."

He gave her a crooked smile. "We-uns got problems, ain't we?"

"But," he added, thoughtfully. "You've got a real hang-up, y'know."

"Like how?" she demanded.

"Like on money."

About to protest hotly, she hesitated, then admitted. "Sure, I'm hung up. But not on a lot of money. Just enough. Enough to make us happy, that's all."

"I wonder how much is enough," he mused, not really asking Lenny but rather himself. "Look at the Blooms. They don't seem to need money or even want it."

His raised hand encircled the glade. "All this, they like the way it is. With Sid's money, he could've built a resort or a hotel. Right?"

Appalled at the idea, Lenny exclaimed, "Oh, no! Gramps wouldn't!"

"Right," Todd agreed. "Gramps wouldn't. Neither would I. What I'd like to do, someday," he continued, "is take up forestry or be a naturalist — something to save all this." He stopped abruptly, looking uncomfortable at his own emotion.

"Yeah," Lenny breathed, not knowing how to say she understood. "Me, too," she said finally. "But I'd like to study animals. Not just tame ones. But wild ones, too." He squeezed her hand. "We'd make a great team, huh? Me, saving the forest. And you, the animals."

His smile, the sharing, the putting into words of her own trouble gave Lenny a feeling of release. She felt suddenly lighter than air. For no reason, a picture of Gram came to mind: Lenny used to watch her while she unwound yards of knotted wool. The yarn, discarded by would-be knitters for the Red Cross, Gram refused to throw away as useless. When she had finished, it was a neat respectable ball, ready once more to be knitted into a pattern. That's exactly the way I feel, Lenny thought, untangled and ready to start afresh.

She turned to Todd with her heart in her eyes. "Thanks," she said. "For listening." Then she smacked his swollen cheek with a spontaneous kiss.

"Ow–ch!" he yelled; then he chuckled at her startled expression.

Suddenly struck by the strangeness of everything, they dissolved in merriment. Laughing at nothing in particular, they clutched at their sides. Todd, with alternate hands, held first his blackened eye and then his stomach. Lenny, mopping at tears on a dust-caked face, managed nothing better than a muddy smear.

The loud clamour of Gram's dinner bell rang through the forest. It clappered across the peninsula and brought them to their senses.

"Dinner?" Lenny asked in amazement. "So soon?"

11 A Letter from Mom

They parted on the "low" path, standing in the exact spot where they'd parted once before. That time, Lenny thought, in anger. This time Todd made no attempt to kiss her, simply holding her hand and asking, "Tonight?"

Lenny nodded; he must know how much she wanted to see him again.

"The crowd's getting together at Ipperwash," he said. "I'll pick you up 'round eight."

"The crowd?"

"Just Barney and Deb. Maybe a few others."

Lenny frowned. "Barney will be there?"

"If you knew Barney, maybe you'd like him."

Lenny was incredulous. "After what happened this afternoon?"

"After what happened this afternoon," he repeated, and Lenny was aware of his double meaning. Todd referred to the glade and their getting to know each other. Lenny, of course, meant her near-accident on the high rocks.

"That's not the same!" she protested. "I sure won't forget what that meathead did to me."

"Neither will I," Todd said. "But I'd like to find out why he did it. Okay?"

Todd was pleading, and Lenny relented. "Okay."

Satisfied, he released her hand, setting off in the opposite direction. "See you at eight," he flung over his shoulder. "Better bring a bikini. We might go swimming."

"I don't own one," Lenny called after him.

"Better bring something or you'll have to skinny-dip. Them's the rules."

Nearing the farmhouse, Lenny experienced a weird sensation of floating. I know, now, she thought, what it means to feel "ten feet tall." The sensation continued right up to the front door where Soapy greeted her in a flurry of skidding paws. "You'd think I'd been to the moon and back," she told him.

"The way you look," Gramps remarked drily, "I'd say that you had." Seated in the leather armchair, newspaper partly lowered, he looked at her teasingly. "What'd you do? Take a Red River cart?"

"Now, Sid," Gram admonished. She was standing in the kitchen doorway and Lenny caught a glimpse of chicken pot pie, its pastry puffed and golden. On the sideboard, sat the salad and beside it jellied desserts shivered lemon-cool under mounds of cream.

"I'm famished," Lenny announced.

"Me too," Gramps echoed. "So let's not take all night getting cleaned up."

Yesterday, his remark might have rankled. But today, Lenny headed for the stairs saying, "Okay. I'll just swish off the grime."

From the bathroom, she could hear Gram berating her husband. "Really, Sid. You might be a little less blunt."

Lenny grinned at his reply. "What for? Why spoil a good dinner. . .while she slathers her face with a pound of guck?" For that, Mr. Bloom, she thought, you'll see me with just soap and water!

At dinner, Lenny's confession that she'd tracked a bobcat — had actually seen one at close quarters brought forth only a mild reaction. Gramps's grunt of disapproval was coupled with the remark, "You're askin' for trouble. Lucky you weren't attacked."

Without thought, Lenny told him, "Somebody scared it off." Then, concentrating on her chicken pie, she added, "Somebody shot off a rifle."

Gramps's fork clanked to the plate. "Summer tourists! No

regard for rules!"

Gram changed the subject. "I meant to tell you, Lenny. There's a letter."

"From Mom and Dad?"

"I imagine so. It's postmarked in the States. Ashland, I think."

"Ashland! But that's just their first stopover. By now, they should be in New York."

"Mail's slow 'round here," Gramps said, leaving Lenny with the unspoken retort, "You can say *that* again!"

Fairly begging to be read, Mom's letter with its familiar handwriting sat propped on the kitchen sill. Finally, unable to wait any longer, Lenny pushed back her chair. "Do you mind?" "I'd like to read it."

Gram gave her an understanding nod. "You go right ahead."

Upstairs, sitting crosslegged on Gram's quilt, Lenny tore open the envelope with unsteady fingers. Oh, gee! she thought. I've missed you guys!

But as she scanned the precise, evenly-spaced words, her excitement cooled. They had kept to their schedule, Mom wrote, reaching Duluth about 5 p.m. It had rained in Iron Mountain and the car was covered with red mud. They expected to reach New York in about a week, stopping off in various places where Dad had made appointments with editors. "Let's hope that they give Daddy the go-ahead," Mom said. "We're practically down to our last nickel. So we might be home sooner than we thought." The letter ended with a reminder to be thoughtful to the Blooms — and to take care.

Lenny folded the letter carefully in its envelope and sat staring at nothing. The airy feeling of elation was gone, replaced by all the old, familiar questions. Was Dad *really* a failure? And, where would they live next? Lenny had no answers, and the knowledge that there weren't any brought a flood of helpless anger and frustration at her inability to help in some small way. She could baby-sit more often, she supposed, but the pay was peanuts. Besides, babysitting kept her up far too late during school week, and she wasn't all that brilliant anyway. I'm a drag, was her dismal thought. Mom and Dad might do much better without me. Nor could she help solve their personal problems. Especially when she couldn't even make up her own mind as to whether she should kiss a guy or not!

Pounding the bedspread with a tight-curled fist, Mom's letter crushed into a ball, Lenny stopped abruptly when Gram called up the stairs. "Todd's here, Lenny. You ready?"

"So soon?"

"It's eight bells, doll," Todd shouted. "If I have to wait — you'd better be beautiful."

Beautiful! Lenny leaped from the bed; she should have shampooed her hair. Nuts! she thought. My first visit to Ipperwash and I wanted to make such a good impression. Now, I'll look what I am — the kid from the wrong side of the tracks!

Thank heaven she still had a clean outfit; white flairs with a matching top that clung to all the proper places. It brightened her eyes and darkened the day's newly acquired tan.

A damp brush brought back some of the hairshine, and some eye shadow and lipstick finished the job. Standing back critically, Lenny thought, not bad — but it could have been better.

Todd stopped his conversation with Gram when Lenny came downstairs. His approving look, one eye still puffy but not so discoloured, was reassuring. "It was worth waiting for," he remarked. "Better bring a sweater, though. And where's the bikini?"

"The what?" Gramps asked.

"A bathing suit," Gram supplied. "In two pieces."

"Huh! One of those nuthin' outfits. Might as well wear your birthday suit!"

Lenny shot an embarrassed look at Todd, but he just grinned.

"I'll get my suit," she said. To Gramps she gave the information that she didn't own a bikini. "Mine's all in one piece." She could have added that the suit was so snug that he'd probably like it less.

But Gramps was off on his favourite subject: the younger generation and what they were coming to. The sooner I get Todd out of here, Lenny thought, the better. Snatching her suit from a bottom drawer, she hurried back downstairs in time to hear Gram's anxious remark, "I've never liked swimming after dark."

Todd's reply was cheerful. "The pier is lighted, Mrs. Bloom. And besides, we have a 'buddy' system."

"What's that?"

"We each have a partner with the same number, and every five minutes we call them out. That way, we can keep track of who's in the water."

"I hope so," Gram said, doubtfully.

Lenny cleared her throat. "I'm ready," she said.

Outside, the air was sweet with night-blooming nicotine, and on the "low" path, the overpowering scent of pine tickled Lenny's nose. She sneezed and had to stop to rummage for a tissue. Aware of Todd's quiet gaze, she wanted more than anything else for him to kiss her. Right now!

"You look terrific," he said.

"In the dark?"

"In white, you're easy to see." He came closer and she raised her face to his.

"Very attractive," he whispered. Then, taking a fast swipe at Lenny's shoulder, he added, "To bugs."

Taken by surprise, angry with herself for mistaking his meaning, Lenny demanded, "What are you doing!"

He laughed. "You had a beetle on your shoulder. I thought you knew that white attracts bugs."

"I can always go back and change," she said.

His arm went about her waist. "No you don't. I like white, too."

The lights of Ipperwash pricked the pines and the sound of music met them as the path smoothed.

"Sounds like the gang is here," Todd said. Taking her hand he began to run — down the flagstone steps flanked by neatly pruned rockeries and round the wide, screened-in veranda to the front entrance. The steps, covered with straw matting, deadened the sound of their arrival.

"Where's Todd — and the new chick?" Barney was asking.

Lenny stiffened, shooting at Todd a silent. "I told you so." But he shook his head and pushed open the door.

"We're here, you lucky people," he announced and pulled Lenny inside.

They sat on bamboo settees or sprawled on outsize cushions scattered about the floor: Debra, flat on her back with head pillowed on Barney's lap, and four others paired off in the flickering shadows of a log fire.

"Meet Lenny O'Hare," Todd said, leading her closer to the fireplace. "My sister Debra. And Barney Mann."

Raising her head from Barney's lap, Debra corrected him sweetly, "Stepsister," and added a brief, "Hi!"

Todd ignored the correction, but Lenny noticed the slight tensing of his hand.

Barney's greeting was more personal, wide smile revealing those white teeth. "About time we got some new scenery," he remarked. Then, to Todd — as if I weren't here! Lenny thought — "The close-up's even better."

"Glad you like it," she said, making no attempt to hide her dislike. Now that she stood face-to-face with Mr. Mann it was almost impossible not to lash out, not to tell him what she thought of him. But instinctively she knew that Todd would want to handle it in his own way, would want to find out why Barney had used a rifle with so little sense. There had to be a very good reason why Todd felt warmth for a person like Barney Mann.

The others, Lenny could barely see. Coupled at either end of a shadowy window seat, they were only names; Jerry McIntosh and Mary Slade, Ray Kerr and Jill Cameron. Lenny recognized some of the names immediately — perhaps from the social pages of the newspaper.

Leading her to a large, fan-backed chair, Todd asked, "Think we can squeeze into this?"

She held back. "I doubt it. Not after Gram's chicken pie."

"The lady's bashful," Barney remarked.

"Or too fat," Debra added.

Barney, eyes on Lenny's snug-fitting top, drawled, "Oh, dunno."

"Okay, Mann!" Todd commanded. "Cut it out."

There was plenty of room in the chair to spare, and Lenny savoured the pleasure of proving Debra wrong. The record player dropped a new disc, filling the room with pulsing sound. Barney began snapping his fingers and swaying, and Debra, sitting up, followed suit, her dark, waist-long hair swinging from side to side. But, so far, Lenny thought, Debra has done nothing to make herself likable.

"Comfortable?" Todd asked.

She smiled at him, resisting an impulse to snuggle, and hearing Mom's oft-repeated advice, "Don't be too obvious, honey. Respect yourself and everyone else will do the same."

"Such a pretty room," Lenny remarked. "What is it about circular rooms?"

She hadn't expected an answer, least of all from Barney. "Didn't you know?" he said. "Circles are endless. You never get lost. You can always get back to where you started."

His remark stirred the memory of a similar one she had overheard that day just below the "high" path. "A loser," Barney had described himself. Barney's hang-up! she thought.

The record ended and Lenny had no brilliant reply. In the silence, from another part of the house, a woman's voice could be heard in husky greeting. "Hi! I thought you could use some company."

And Barney, sounding overly harsh, remarked, "There's Mom. Come for her usual nightcap."

Debra, springing to her feet, announced brightly, "Time for a swim." Ignoring the chorus of protest, she ordered, "Gals undress in my room. Boys in Todd's"

"Phooey!" Todd whispered. "I was just getting cosy."

Lenny sighed. "Me too."

12 Buddy Number Two

Following Debra down a green-carpeted hall, Lenny caught a glimpse of a large, high-ceilinged bathroom, pale pink and hung with carnation-red towels. There was even a glassed-in shower stall. What a summer home! she thought. It seems more like a mansion.

Prettier than any bedroom Lenny could remember, Debra's was furnished in Early American maple, the floor covered with a deep-pile rug. The dresser, Lenny noticed, was crowded with lipsticks and expensive perfumes. The lipsticks alone, Lenny thought, would take every cent of her allowance for at least a year!

"Make yourselves at home," Debra told them. "I'll be back in a minute. I want to talk to Barney."

Mary, a tall blonde girl began unzipping her slacks. "Barney's been into the juice at the Brewster bar," she commented. "Guess it runs in the family."

Jill, struggling with back buttons, asked, "You mean drinking, I suppose?"

Mary nodded. "His mother's an alcoholic, isn't she?"

Jill shrugged, glancing at Lenny who stood hesitant about getting undressed in front of strangers. She wasn't used to it; the few times she'd done it, she'd always flamed with embarrassment. But Jill, stepping out of her underwear, stood plump and full-breasted, seemingly unconcerned. Her face was friendly.

"Sorry, Lenny. Ignore the back-fence gossip. But this summer, Barney is a kind of 'gang' problem. Personally, I don't know why we don't just tell him so."

Mary snorted, "Well, I do. The little rich kid's mixed up enough without us playing 'shrink.' "

Jill turned on her. "That may be your reason. But it sure-as-heck isn't mine. Barney used to be a real nice guy. We should at least try to straighten him out."

Lenny, feeling out of the conversation, draped her suit over a shoulder and headed for the bathroom.

"Hey!" Mary jeered. "Todd's little friend is shy."

"Oh, can it!" Jill snapped as Lenny closed the door.

"I don't know how to act with these girls," Lenny groaned. "I'm just not one of them."

Debra's voice came clearly from the next room. "Guess what?" she said. "I was just entertaining a Forest Ranger. He wanted to know if we'd heard any rifle shots this morning."

"What did you tell him?" Mary asked. "The truth?"

" 'Course not. Barney just did it for kicks. Why get him into trouble?"

Lenny's hands clenched on her suit strap.

So they all *knew* about the shooting! And they were lying to the law! Damn them, anyway. If Todd didn't do something, she would. Who did these creeps think they were?

A quick glance in the full-length mirror satisfied Lenny that her suit fitted to perfection. Then she opened the door, ready to do battle. But the room was empty; her hostess and guests had not bothered to wait.

In the hallway, two women stood talking. The tall one with silver-blonde hair could be no one else but Todd's mother. The resemblance was marked. The other woman, dark and painfully thin, Lenny had not seen before. In the dimly-lit passageway, her face looked putty-coloured and her eyes deeply circled.

The tall woman held out a hand and smiled. "You must be Lenny," she said. "I'm Todd's mother. We've been hearing a lot about Lenny O'Hare. I was wondering when we'd meet."

"How do you do," Lenny said, wishing she could manage something less stilted. Mrs. Brewster had the dignity and poise of

84

an experienced hostess and the thought flickered briefly that Debra could certainly have no criticism of her step-mother in that area.

Mrs. Brewster was introducing her friend. "This is Mrs. Mann, Barney's mother. Their cottage is just next door."

Lenny offered her hand, and knew immediately that it was a mistake. Mrs. Mann held a too-full glass in one hand, a cigarette in the other.

She nodded. "Nice to meet-chew." Barney's mother, Lenny thought, certainly didn't need any nightcap. The whole hallway reeked of liquor!

From the sunporch, Todd was asking, "Where's Lenny?"

"You're being paged," Mrs. Brewster said, standing aside to let Lenny pass. "Maybe after your swim, we can talk. Todd tells me your father is a writer. I'd like to hear more."

Lenny's heart sank. I wonder what Todd has told her, she thought; hurrying toward the sound of general exodus, she heard Mrs. Brewster suggest to Mrs. Mann, "Maybe you'd like a cup of coffee?" "Don't bother, dear." Mrs. Mann replied, "I have all I want — right here."

On the veranda, Todd sat alone, perched on the arm of a chair. He turned when he heard her, his smile belying his words. "About time," he said. "I thought I'd lost my 'buddy' number."

Lenny looked at him blankly. "Your what?"

"The buddy system," he explained. "When we're in swimming. Our number is two." He laughed, pulling her to his side. "If we're separated, we answer with good old number two."

Standing there, with Todd's arm about her shoulder, Lenny felt his closeness, his too-positive assurance that he had it made. Two conflicting emotions fought within her, the overwhelming urge to press closer, and the feeling that she should pull away. Not knowing which to heed, she simply stiffened and stood still.

Todd, looking down, became suddenly serious. "You don't like?"

"Yes," she admitted honestly. "But I don't know."

"What's that supposed to mean?"

Lenny gave him a helpless smile. "I don't know," she repeated, and his hand dropped abruptly.

Todd's eyes, almost colourless in the moonlight shafting through the screen, searched her face. "Some buddy!" he said, and began running down the fir-shadowed path to the dock.

Picking her way slowly from one flagstone to the next, Lenny thought, I've hurt his feelings. He probably thinks I'm a zero. She could hear the hollow pounding of Todd's feet on the planked dock and Barney's yell, "Hey! Look out for the blond bomber!" Then the groaning twang of a diving board and a loud splash. Her "buddy," it appeared, was the first in the water.

Someone switched on the boathouse lights. They bloomed in a brilliant yellow necklace as Lenny stepped onto the dock. Blinded for a moment, she shaded her eyes. Someone else gave a long wolf-whistle, and Debra's voice sang with cutting sweetness. *Ta-dada-da — tadah!*"

The hurt, the inference that Lenny had made a planned entrance, was suddenly more than she could bear. Feet quickening, without a word, she followed Todd, aware of six pairs of eyes, and exulting briefly in her own professional dive. Under the water, she expelled her breath in long necklaces of bubbles while invisible weeds trailed slimy fingers along her legs. Finally the dark, liquid loneliness brought her shuddering to the surface. Emerging on the moon-shaded side of the boathouse, she felt washed clean of temper. Her hair floating loose about her face and shoulders reminded her that she'd forgotten to tie it up. That'll teach me to get into such a snit, she thought ruefully. Now I'll look like a witch for the rest of the evening.

Above the sucking thump of the cruiser swaying against her moorings, Lenny could hear the conversation on the dock. She enjoyed a perverse pleasure in remaining silent.

"That gal must have great lungs," Barney said. "Where'd she go?"

"An Irish temper, too," Mary added.

"I 'yike,' " Barney quipped, and Lenny grinned at Debra's instant reaction.

"That, Barney Mann, is your last drink," she told him firmly. "A few drinks and you're off your nut."

There was the sound of a scuffle, and Barney's exclamation, "Hey, gimme back my glass!" Then, a small, gurgling splash when something was either thrown or dropped into the lake.

Not twenty feet away, Todd, who must have been treading water, called, "Who just dived?"

"It was Lenny," Jill told him. "Isn't she out there."

There was a short, searching silence. Then, Todd's voice trumpeted about the bay, "Buddy Number Two calling! Answer me, Number Two!"

Why she did it, let herself sink silently beneath the surface, Lenny could not explain. Do I want to frighten someone? Do I want that someone to care? I'm an idiot, she told herself. Todd will be furious.

The moment Lenny thrashed to the surface gasping, "Here!" Todd was heading in the direction of her voice, arms cutting the water with short, angry strokes.

She waited: the jarring thud of his body not unexpected, his opinion of her behaviour certainly justified.

"You idiot!" he shouted, fingers gripping her shoulders, making her wince. They sank together, feet touching bottom and chins barely above water.

"Why?" he demanded, and Lenny could only shake her head.

"For kicks?" he asked, not attempting to disguise his disgust.

"Maybe," she whispered, aware that they stood in bright moonlight and were watched by an interested audience from the now-silent dock. The word, "kicks," had a familiar ring and Lenny realized its association with Barney Mann. Someone who specialized in kicks — and someone she despised!

"Sorry," she said. "Truly I am."

Todd's expression softened — at least, Lenny imagined that it did — and trying to smile, she managed only to wobble her lips.

"Lenny," he commanded quietly. "Don't *ever* do that again."

"I won't," she promised solemnly, and breaking away, she made for the dock.

The ladder steps were slippery and Lenny floundered at the dock's edge. Accepting Barney's helping hand, she heaved herself upward with a mighty splash, to be greeted with a chorus of dismayed yelps. "Hey! Watch it! Help!"

"Make way," she said, "for one dumb dame."

"You can say that again," Debra commented.

"Not so dumb," Barney said. "We can always use a little excitement."

"How's about some water-skiing?" he asked brightly.

Clinging to the ladder, Todd replied sharply. "No water-skiing between sunset and sunrise. It's a criminal offence."

"Oh pshaw!" Mary said.

"Skip it," Debra told Barney. "Toddy's just been boning up on all his water regulations."

A small breeze scurried across the lake, fuzzing the surface. Lenny shivered. "I left my towel," she said, "back at the house."

"Here," Jill offered. "You can share mine."

"Thanks," Lenny said. "But I have to dry my hair. Yours would get sopped. I'd better get my own."

Hurrying back up the path, she thought, I don't like them. And the feeling seems to be mutual. I just *don't* belong. A misjudged flagstone and a stubbed toe brought her abruptly to her knees.

"Damnation!" she muttered.

Todd, directly behind her, chimed in, "Temper! temper!"

Checking a rude retort, Lenny told herself that Todd was hardly to blame for her own nutty behaviour. Nor, for that matter, was he to blame for the actions of his friends. As if reading her thoughts, he said, "The crowd's not always like this. So don't judge us too quickly."

"I guess," Lenny admitted slowly, "I didn't make such a good impression myself."

The veranda lights caught his grin. "Nope," he agreed. Lenny laughed, smacking a wet hand on his bare shoulder and leaping for the steps.

Stretched on a wicker lounge and holding a glass with both

hands, Barney's mother raised her eyes from the drink.

"Youth," she remarked, blurrily. "Youth and love. Can't have one — without the other."

Under his breath, Todd muttered, "Oh, brother!" Then, aloud, he asked, "Where's Mom, Mrs. Mann?"

Turning to Lenny, he said, "See you later. Looks as if Mom might need me."

His bleak expression brought a pang of sympathy. "Couldn't I . . .?" Lenny began. But he shook his head. "You go dry your hair."

Standing her ground, Lenny persisted. "Why you?" she asked. "Why not Mr. Mann? Barney's father?"

Thoughtlessly, she had forgotten that she might be heard — and understood. Todd's warning look came too late.

Mrs. Mann gave a harsh exclamation. "Hah! That's a good question!"

"Please Lenny," Todd pleaded. "You'll only make things worse."

"Sorry," she said tonelessly, and headed for the bedroom. Why can't I do *anything* right? she asked herself.

Towelling her head roughly, tugging at tangled hair and pinning it into a roll, Lenny scowled at her mirrored reflection. Without even trying, she thought, I've managed to start a wonderful evening in the worst way possible.

13 Satan's Gorge

Lenny stood at the window in Debra's darkened room reluctant to join in the group down on the dock, especially without Todd. Nor did she want to risk another meeting with Mrs. Mann.

The window opened on a quiet back bay, a tree-laced crescent of moonlight. For the moment, no voices broke the stillness; there was only the lapping gurgle of the lake and the soft sounds of night. Far off, the sweet whirling melody of a veery — *vee-ur, vee-ur, vee-ur* — rang through the woods. Lenny held her breath, listening as each pure note spiralled downward, lower, lower, and then was gone, leaving an embroidered silence.

Accustomed now to the darkness, Lenny caught the twinkling flash of fireflies on the far bank. Their tiny, blue-green lanterns blinked love-messages to each other. She smiled, remembering when she was six and had first visited the Blooms. Fireflies, she'd insisted, were really Tinker Bells. Clinging to the fantasy of Barrie's "Peter Pan", she had refused to believe Gramps when he told her that fireflies were beetles with lights in their tails.

From the hallway, came the sound of low voices, and Lenny made a move to let Todd and his mother know of her presence. Their conversation was not meant for Lenny's ears.

"I can't send her home," Mrs. Brewster was protesting. "Sally Mann is an old friend."

Todd sounded firm. "I know, Mom. But letting her drink all our booze isn't helping anything. Either cut off her drinks or let me take her home."

In the darkened bedroom, Lenny squirmed, feeling like an

eavesdropper. Which I am, she thought. But what else can I do?

Mrs. Brewster was weakening. "We-ll," she said. "If you think you can do it politely."

"Get real, Mom. Your friend lost her manners about three snorts ago. No wonder her husband takes off."

"That's enough, Todd. You can't know the circumstances."

"Well, I know *one* thing," he whispered, loudly. "I can see what it's doing to Barney."

"Barney isn't helping the situation either —"

I don't want to hear, Lenny decided. Tiptoeing to Debra's bathroom, she closed the door. Once inside, Lenny turned on the light, flushed the toilet, and splashed tap-water noisily into the basin. Then waiting for a suitable few minutes, she made her exit.

Reaching the hallway, Lenny found it empty, and on the veranda Mrs. Brewster sat alone. "Oh, there you are," she said. "Todd asked me to tell you he's escorting Mrs. Mann home. At night, you know, the path is pretty dark."

Lenny returned her smile, knowing her own to be artificial and wondering if her expression would betray what she had heard.

"Sit down, dear," Mrs. Brewster said, indicating a stool at her feet. "Maybe we can have that little chat. I'd love to hear more about your father. What he writes. Where I can get his books."

Wishing she could turn and run, Lenny sat down reluctantly. "Dad doesn't write books. I mean. . .," she stammered, "he writes books. But they haven't been published."

Her face in shadow, Mrs. Brewster replied quietly, "Oh, I see."

No, Lenny wanted to say, you *don't* see! You can't possibly know how hard my father works. How hard it is to keep on believing. She could hear again Dad's rueful remark, "I guess, Lenny, writers have to be blockheads. Or stubborn Irishmen like me."

"He writes mostly articles," Lenny continued. "For well-known magazines like *Macleans* — and *Atlantic*." She lowered her eyes, bending to scratch at an imaginary mosquito bite. "You're lying," her conscience said, sternly. "Your father has sold only once to *Atlantic*."

"Not very often to *Atlantic*," Lenny admitted miserably. "Dad's having a rough time. That's why my parents are down in the States. Dad's trying to make more contacts." Blinking in the lamplight, she stared defiantly at her hostess.

"You're proud of your father, aren't you?" Mrs. Brewster said softly.

"Yes."

"Then you don't have to worry," she replied. "With a daughter like you, any father is a success."

Lenny's throat became suddenly clogged, too full to say even "Thank you." She had not been aware of her own pride.

Unheard, Todd had come in the back door. "What'd I tell you?" he said. "When I pick 'em, I *pick* 'em."

Lenny laughed, glad to be pulled roughly to her feet, glad to have her emotions back where they belonged.

"Where's the sharp bathing suit?" he demanded. "No more swimming?"

"Too cold," she said. "And too wet."

"Yeah," he agreed. "I was going to change to something dry, myself." He brightened. "Let's take a spin in *The Scotsman*."

Lenny hesitated. Gram and Gramps disapproved of night boating. Even Dad admitted honestly that navigating among so many islands required an excellent mariner, especially after dark.

"Why don't you," urged Mrs. Brewster. "On a night like this, the lake is never lovelier. You'll be perfectly safe with Todd. He's the only one my husband trusts with the cruiser after nightfall."

"All right," Lenny said. "I'd love to."

Nearing the dock, they could hear hysterical laughter, the rhythmic clap of hands, and Barney's raucous voice singing.

"Clown," Todd remarked, and beneath the dry comment, Lenny detected his fondness.

Barney's audience, backs propped against the boathouse wall, sat two by two under blankets. Only Debra sat alone, perched on the diving board, seemingly undaunted by the cooling breeze.

"Hey! You guys anti-social?" she called.

"Yep," Todd said. "We're leaving. I'm taking Lenny out for a spin."

"Me too," she said, teetering to her feet on the board. "How's about it, gang?"

But the "gang" was too comfortable, and Todd had other plans. "Just Lenny and me. This is her first trip."

Debra snorted, but she accepted Todd's ultimatum with a friendly pout. "Big wheel," she remarked. "Just because Papa's made you responsible."

Helping Lenny aboard, Todd ignored his stepsister. "You check the lights, Lenny," he ordered. "Green for starboard. That's on your right. Red lights on the port side. White at stern and bow."

"Okay?" he shouted, and at her nod, he bent down to check the life-jackets under the seats.

Barney had stopped his singing to watch, face comically deadpan. "Hey, skipper!" he yelled. "What about the squirt-gun? For Fires."

Todd grinned and patted the extinguisher. "Roger!" he called, then throttled the motor.

The cruiser skimmed on quicksilver, every island merging deceptively into a single inky shoreline. Lenny, straightening on the deep-cushioned seat, peered through the windshield. "How do we know where we're going?"

"Simple," Todd told her. "See this point of land? This is the Mann's place, the one with the white summerhouse."

Lenny spotted the small structure, perched on its rocky platform, resembling a plump tea-cosy.

"Just keep the stern on the summerhouse," Todd explained. "And this," he tapped the steering wheel, running a finger down its top spoke, "you keep in line with the flag on the bow."

"Takes you straight to the nearest channel buoy," he continued. "Here I'll show you. Move closer and you can do it yourself."

When Lenny shook her head, he found her hand and placed it on the wheel. Power throbbed beneath her palm and she threw him a frightened glance as the boat swerved immediately off course.

"Keep the wheel-spoke in line with the flag," he directed. " 'S perfectly safe — outside of other boats and dead-heads."

"Dead-heads?"

He laughed. "Logs floating vertically in the water."

"Oh, no," Lenny pleaded. "You steer."

Taking the wheel again, Todd nodded up ahead. "See, what did I tell you. There's your channel marker. You can't miss."

Leaning back with a relieved sigh, Lenny said, "Like father, like daughter. No sense of direction." "No sense," she added. "Period."

Bending unexpectedly, Todd planted a brief kiss on her cheek. "That last remark," he told her, "you can scratch."

Impulsively Lenny pressed against him, fitting her head into the curve of his shoulder, and holding his arm with both hands. He glanced down, voice unsteady. "Hey. You're sending me." Lenny pulled away, sliding the length of the seat, and feeling ridiculous. I used to snuggle that way with Dad she thought, confused. Todd's hands on the wheel, their competent strength, gave her the same sense of security. But, this . . . was so different!

Todd concentrated on the next buoy, their lights picking out a black finger rearing up to starboard. At closer range, Lenny noticed that it was not black, but red. "We must be travelling upstream," she announced.

"Good girl. You're learning fast. Red markers on the starboard. Black ones on the port side."

Up ahead, an island seemed suddenly to break away from the mainland, a strip of moon-splashed water leading to a dark hole in what appeared to be unbroken rock. Tacked on either side, two brilliant lights assured Lenny that it was, indeed, a waterway.

"Satan's Gorge," Todd said, slowing the motor. Steering carefully for the twin lights, he remarked, "Hope we don't meet *The Princess*. It's about time for her return trip."

Lenny hoped so, too. *The Princess*, a wide paddlewheeler for sightseeing tourists, plied Black Rock Lake three times a day.

94

Together, *The Scotsman* and *The Princess* could hardly squeeze through such a small entrance.

As if to prove the danger, Satan's evil face painted on a monstrous egg-shaped rock leaped into view. The fanged mouth, the soulless eyes, laughed at their temerity. Lenny shuddered.

With a tingling sense of unease she recalled the distant view of it from the ledge at the bobcat's cave. Then it seemed to mock her; now it seemed only to emphasize how badly she managed everything — particularly Todd.

"It's just an Indian spirit rock," Todd informed her. "Even today the Indians put offerings at its base — insurance for good crops and plenty of fish."

"With that face?"

Todd laughed. "The face is the white man's idea. Back in the 1890's, some of the boys from town went on a beer-drinking spree and painted the face for kicks. Now the Department of Transport does it — with paint left over from the channel buoys. But some of the real Indian picture rocks look just as fresh as the day they were painted."

Lenny recalled what Gramps had told her about Indian picture rocks and how the paint — a mixture of berry juice, spruce gum, fish oils and minerals — never seemed to fade. But the recollections made the Satan's Gorge face even more unnatural and ominous.

"I don't like it, Todd," she said quietly.

The comment went unnoticed. The hoarse bellow of *The Princess* suddenly rocketted about the gorge and Lenny stiffened, sending Todd a wide-eyed question.

"We can make it," he assured her. "She's still at the other end of the narrows."

The Scotsman, easing through the narrow entrance, seemed dangerously close to the rocky overhang. Then, without reason, the cruiser lost her buoyancy, sagging heavily in the water, stopping — pulsing unevenly — beginning again.

"What is it?" Lenny exclaimed.

"Weird, huh? Does it every time. It's the pull of the current, I guess. The water's only twenty feet deep as you enter, then eighty feet the moment you're inside."

"Creepy," Lenny agreed.

"The Indians think so, too," Todd said. "You'll never see an Indian enter the gorge in midstream. They always hug the far shore.

"I don't blame them," Lenny replied.

The Princess, plump passage bulging the narrows with wash, hove into view. Her lighted decks sprayed the shore with brilliance, casting living patterns on the rocks.

Suddenly overcome with the beauty, Lenny crossed her arms over her breasts, hands pressing hard against her ribs to control the tremor. The tremor was no chill; she had never felt so warmly alive. Every sense tingled — to the velvet brush of the air singing through the cabin vents; to the lemon light of the dashboard fuzzing Todd's lean, bare thighs.

Despite the devil's face, despite the gang at the dock, despite her mother's wise advice, Lenny felt deliriously happy. She knew she wanted Todd, wanted him to know her and like her, and to show it — now! Almost unconsciously she snuggled up against him and put her hand on his arm.

"Don't *do* that!" Todd almost shouted.

Lenny sprang back in a muddle of confusion and dismay.

"What's the matter with you, Lenny. When the time is right, I can't even get near you. But here, with *The Princess* almost on top of us, you decide to get cosy. Satan's Gorge isn't exactly lover's lane you know."

The silence that followed was broken by the growing thunder of *The Princess*. Then her bulk churned by them in a torrent of spray. Lenny just sat at her end of the seat, hurt and suddenly angry.

Even if I did move at the wrong time, she told herself, a moment of almost unbelievable beauty had been shattered by Todd's insensitivity. Only one or two tender words were all that were needed — not a stupid outburst.

As the roar of *The Princess* diminished, Todd turned to her, his voice on the point of laughter. "I can cut the motor and drift now if you like."

Lenny was almost astonished by the coldness of her reply. "Don't bother," she grated. "After all, it's dangerous here."

Todd sat up straight and pushed the throttle. As *The Scotsman* made a clean half-turn, striping the inky water with luminous foam, he responded with exaggerated politeness: "If the inclination ever strikes you again, I can think of better places. . .Miss O'Hare."

Lenny remained silent, not daring to speak, tears dimming the retreating lights of *The Princess*. For a crazy moment, all she could think of was the devil's face out there in the darkness — laughing at her.

"This is what I've waited for. This is what Todd waited for. And it's all been spoilt," Lenny railed to herself. And she knew it would be a long time before either of them could even mention the incident without releasing a torrent of resentment and misunderstanding. In her misery, the problem of wandering parents, a cat-napped kitten — even trigger-happy Barney Mann — were driven from her mind.

14 A Close Call for Barney

But Barney Mann, it seemed, was one problem not so easily dismissed.

When Ipperwash sparkled into sight, Lenny felt immensely relieved. Unable to think of anything to say, she had remained silent, wishing she could erase everything that had been said.

Todd had not spoken either. Eyes straight ahead, he hurled *The Scotsman* toward the distant lights. As if, Lenny concluded miserably, he can't *wait* to reach shore! For what? she wondered. To drop me flat?

"Sheesh!" he exclaimed, shattering Lenny's mood. "Look at that weirdo!"

The "weirdo," alias Barney Mann, perched on the edge of the dock. Water skis dangling and towline tautening, he was about to take off behind an outboard.

Cutting the cruiser's motor, Todd leaned across Lenny to peer out the window. For a brief moment, Barney's seat seemed glued to the dock. Then, as the outboard gained momentum, he came unstuck — white trunks flapping in ribboned distress and water boiling in his wake.

Todd clapped a hand to his head. "My new trunks!" he bawled, "he ripped the seat right out of them." Lenny collapsed with merriment. Through tears of laughter, she could see the people on the dock pointing and gesticulating like puppets.

From the drifting cruiser, they quickly lost sight of the fluttering shorts. Only the outboard's snarl as it circled in open water told them that Barney still remained on skis.

"Now's our chance to dock," Todd said. "Before those dough-heads get back." The words had barely left his lips when the outboard sputtered to a stop. "Barney's off. Just what he needs — a cold shower. Boy!" he added. "I oughtta clobber that guy!"

Lenny didn't hear. "Something's wrong!" she exclaimed. Concerned calls of "Barney! Hey, Mann!" came clearly across the water. Debra, a yellow exclamation point, stood poised on the diving board.

Unperturbed, Todd started the engine, manoeuvring the cruiser in line with her anchorage. "So Barney got dunked," he said. "Floating around in a life-jacket should sober him up."

"Barney wasn't wearing a jacket."

Todd gave a superior smile. "The outboard's full of safety cushions." He nodded toward the boathouse. "Besides, there goes Debbie to the rescue."

"How can you be so sure?" Lenny demanded. "Anyway, I thought Barney was your friend."

Todd's calmness was infuriating. "Look, there's five people to look after Barney." He patted the wheel. "But only me to look after *The Scotsman*."

"To hell with *The Scotsman*!" Lenny blazed, snatching at the wheel and attempting to change course. But Todd was quicker. One hand clamped about her wrist, the other firmly guiding the cruiser, he asked, coolly, "Just what did you have in mind?"

Deflated, Lenny replied, "Throw Barney a life-jacket, I guess. Not just sit here." In the light from the dashboard, his eyes were expressionless. This was another Todd; one Lenny had not seen. This was a boy who seemed to value possessions more than a friend's safety. That's unfair, Lenny argued silently. Todd ought to know if there are cushions in the outboard. And, he *is* responsible for *The Scotsman*.

Maybe that was the key for Todd's unreasonable behaviour she decided. *The Scotsman* is his stepfather's most cherished possession and Todd's main chance to impress at least one member of the Brewster family. But even that could not excuse his lack of concern for Barney. "I still think," she insisted stubbornly, "we should check."

Todd cut the motor and leaned back. "Go ahead," he said. "Check."

Unaware that they had come so close, Lenny saw the outboard bobbing nearby and heard Mary's urgent call, "Hey, Todd! Throw us a jacket. Our cushions are water-logged. Barney got clonked on the head and Deb's having trouble."

Todd exploded into action. Snapping a jacket from beneath the seat, he jack-knifed through the cabin door leaving Lenny with a terse, "Hold her steady." A quiet splash from the stern and he was gone.

Clinging to the wheel, Lenny wondered what she should do if the cruiser drifted too close to the outboard. If the necessity arose, she had no idea how to start the motor. Unable to watch what was happening, she concentrated on keeping the bow pointed at a sentinel pine, wondering all the while how long it would be before the cruiser lost its momentum and could not be directed at all. Suddenly the other boat crackled to life. Helplessly she heard it approach and winced at the grating bump as it came alongside. "Now, what!" she cried.

"Nothing," Todd grunted, scrambling aboard in a spray of drops. "Barney's okay. But we can't get him aboard. We're going to tow him and Deb ashore."

Lenny made no comment. Todd scraped his throat self-consciously. "Go ahead," he said. "Say it."

But Lenny said nothing. Let him squirm, she thought, just let him squirm. Squirm Todd did — all through the slow trip to the dock, the struggle to help a subdued Barney up the ladder and the search for towels and blankets to make him more comfortable. He was still silent while everyone was noisily thinking of a reasonable explanation for the rapidly swelling bruise on Barney's forehead.

"He dived and hit bottom," was Mary's brilliant suggestion.

"I'm a drip," Barney mumbled. Nobody disagreed.

He looked so miserable that Lenny's heart flooded with

sympathy. For a fleeting moment, she was reminded of Mittens. Last summer, trying to rid the cat of fleas, Lenny had dunked her in the washtub. Mittens had come out resembling a "pipe cleaner" toy rather than a cat.

"I'm a stupid drip," Barney repeated, and Lenny knelt at his side.

"Yes," she agreed. "You are. You gave us a terrible scare."

Barney smiled, weakly. "Yeah?"

"Yeah," Todd broke in. "You can thank Lenny for the life-jacket. Why she wants to save a guy who nearly shot her this afternoon. . ."

Barney's eyes opened incredulously. "What're you beatin' your gums about?"

"Todd," Lenny pleaded. "Not now."

"Take a good look at her," Todd commanded. "Then get out your picturebook on bobcats."

Barney turned to Lenny, face drawn with dismay. She nodded, dumbly, and he paled. Then, to her horror, he crumpled, head bowed over bent knees, shuddering.

Touching his towel-draped shoulder, Lenny whispered, "Barney, it was an accident. A mistake."

In the uncomfortable silence, someone remarked, "He's punchy, I guess. From the bump."

"I hope," Debra snapped, "you two are satisfied."

"Yeah," Mary said.

"Yeah," Gerry echoed.

But Todd, still on the defensive, shot back, "It's about time everybody stopped covering for this guy."

Debra's small face contorted with anger. "Okay," she ordered. "Party's over. Goodnight all."

Lenny got slowly to her feet, and Todd, leading the way to the house, said, "Come on. I have to change."

The others followed silently, drifting in couples up various paths, then disappearing.

Waiting outside on the straw-matted step, Lenny thought over the confusing events. It was partly my fault, she decided ruefully.

I was so furious about Barney that I convinced Todd that his friend should be punished. But Barney had been punishing himself. Why? To hurt his mother in the hope that she'd care? None of it seemed to make sense. Even I, Lenny concluded, played at drowning tonight. Just to see if Todd would be concerned.

Chin propped on a hand, forehead creased in puzzlement, she did not hear Todd till he spoke. "Solving the problems of the world?"

Irritated by his flippant tone, she blurted, "*Somebody* has to care!"

"About Barney, you mean?" Without waiting for an answer, Todd said, "We all care about that guy. Trouble is, we can't get through. I tried down there on the dock. I guess I was too rough."

"You want my opinion?"

At his nod, she said, "I think you were. But, maybe you timed it right."

He snorted, "Timed! I was only sounding off because of a certain girl."

Lenny looked innocent. "Who? Me?"

He pulled her to her feet. "Yeah, you. How do you handle a dame who dummies up? Blow your stack? Or take her home?"

"You've already blown your stack," she reminded him.

He grinned, knuckling a fist under her chin. "Let's go," he said.

15 ⓂMoonlit Glade

Not till they mounted the flagstone steps leading to the "low" path, did Lenny recall the exchange at Satan's Gorge. "Not here!" she'd said, followed by Todd's reply, "I can think of a better place." Strangely, she no longer felt embarrassment.

Beneath their feet, the earth roughened as the path vanished in velvet shade. Lenny hung back. "Didn't you bring a lantern?"

"Yup," he said, and pulled out a pencil flashlight, its slender beam a mere thread. " 'Fraid of the dark?" he teased.

I don't know, she thought, confused. I honestly don't know! But she matched her stride with his, following the flickering dance of the beam. Like a firefly, Lenny mused, glowing, beckoning, always out of reach.

Then it held steady, a disc of gold centred in the heart of the ancient up-ended tree. Looking like an underwater monster, the twisted roots seemed to warn them off as Todd slowed to a stop.

"Well?" he said, and Lenny sensed his meaning. Off to the right branched the trail to the glade with the steps leading to nowhere, and the magic of moon and night. Always before, the glade had belonged to Lenny alone. But now she could share it with Todd.

Flickering off the flash, he waited, silent, letting the night wash over them — neither tightening his hold on her waist, nor loosening it. A breeze wound through the tree-crowns leaving a tiny sound track: a slither of falling needles, a rustle of leaves, one sulky chirp from a roosting bird.

Briefly, Lenny bent her cheek to Todd's shoulder as the

103

flashlight again pricked the path. Quickly they followed its beam, brittle cones exploding underfoot, tangled sumac clutching at their legs. Without a word, Todd led the way with Lenny stumbling in the rear. A mosquito whined in shrill insolence and Lenny smacked at it, losing her balance in the darkness. Too fast! she thought in panic. Todd's going too fast. I *won't* go!

But, turning, he lighted the way for her feet, hand out-stretched to help. "C'mon, stumble-bum," he whispered. "We're here."

Later, when Lenny wondered about not turning back, the memory of that moment by the upturned tree was important. Todd, too, sensed the magic of the glade. But now, seeing his big silhouette framed in the leafy opening, her hand fluttered indecisively away from his proffered clasp.

"Look, Lenny," he whispered. "Look!"

Her fears dissolved. Hand curled in his, she went to the edge of the clearing. The glade has been waiting, she thought tremulously, for just this time. She breathed deeply, marvelling at the beauty of the spot when the lingering warmth of the day was misted cool by the moon.

In the strange light, scarlet bunchberry gleamed ebony, plum and wild sweet pea shone waxen-pale. The daisies, Lenny noted, had petals partly open: yellow eyes playing peek-a-boo in a make-believe dawn.

The sad call of a white-throated sparrow began, then stopped in confusion. Should he sing a morning carol? Or perhaps an evening vesper?

Lenny raised her eyes to Todd. "Glad you came?" he asked, and she nodded wordlessly, letting him lead her to the great rock where they had sat that day at noon.

At first, seated side by side, shoulders touching and legs outstretched, they were quiet. Lenny, leaning back with palms on cool moss, became suddenly aware of Todd's leg running the length of her own. Not touching, but too close — too warm. Sniffing loudly, she filled her nose with the strong aroma of an unknown plant. "What is it?" she asked, not expecting Todd to know.

"Tansy," he replied quickly. As if he, too, was glad to say anything at all. "Dad used to be a wildflower nut," he explained. "That's how I know."

"Oh"

The silence grew big again, making each breath a labour of sound. "Isn't there a tansy tea?" Lenny asked in desperation, remembering what Gram had once told her.

Todd didn't answer. He just looked at her — hard and long. Abruptly, she threw back her head, loosening her hair, wanting to meet his eyes, yet yearning to wing away — up there in the star-spun sky.

"Lenny?" he said. And, she could hardly hear for the thunder in her head. "Keep your head," the poem went, "when all about you, others . . ." But there weren't any others. Only herself and Todd. Todd repeating "Lenny," — her name so lovely she could hardly bear its sound.

Wide-eyed, Lenny saw the stars blur, then mesh. Some had already fallen, glittering at the edge of the glade. Fireflies, she told herself. Love-twinkles all around. But there were only two, spaced evenly a foot above the ground. And not moving.

She tensed. Arms which had threatened collapse suddenly rooted strong fingers anchored in the moss. Todd, sensing the change, started to lift his head. But against his temple, Lenny's lips sent a message, "Bobcat! Don't move!"

The cat — there was no mistaking that tip-tilted eyeshine — seemed unsure of the situation. No wonder, Lenny thought. Her mouth curved, tasting the salt of Todd's skin. Slowly he turned his head, cheek against hers, and together they watched, barely breathing.

The eyes remained unblinking, green-gold and inscrutable. A cool shiver scampering up Lenny's spine raised a crop of goose pimples. I'm *not* afraid, she told herself, sturdily. Bobcats rarely attack. They're people-haters and would rather leave us alone. But why doesn't *this* one leave?

A breeze quivered some hemlock and the reason suddenly

appeared: the kitten bounced into the glade, its mother uttering a high note of admonishment. Then she, too, slid into sight. In full view, they were both beautiful, terrible creatures of the night. Triangular ears brushed with black; full-furred cheeks antennaed with white; black-satin smiles stilettoed with teeth. The mother listened, looked, and seemed satisfied. Turning her head, she called the kitten.

Lenny, relaxing against Todd, was reassured that he would remain still, watching like herself. She could feel his contained amusement as the kitten, in haphazard imitation, bumbled behind its mother. The youngster, plopping a paw on an imaginary prey, scrambled beneath a branch instead of over, fell sadly behind his teacher, then caught up while she waited. As they skirted the edge of the glade, their barred and spotted forms melted half-in, half-out of the shadows. Gone too soon, Lenny thought. This lovely forest duet would be only a dream, something to cherish like this moment with Todd. A coming-together, she concluded, overflowing with beauty.

A twig snapped, and the air, suddenly cool, drenched the woodland pocket. Noiselessly the mother cat sank to her belly, forepaws outstretched; the kitten, a few feet distant, mimicked her fluid movement. Lenny shivered, feeling the slight pressure of Todd's cheek as his eyes swung to another part of the glade.

A rabbit, plump and richly brown, sat at the circle's edge. Then, in true Disney-fashion, it proceeded to do all the adorable things that bunnies are supposed to do.

Entranced, Lenny watched a nose-wiggle, an ear-twitch and a rapid, once-over face wash. Then with a quick right-about hop, the rabbit presented its fat bottom to the cats and began nibbling its way back into the forest.

Todd sucked in his breath — and Lenny froze. A blurred form in mid-flight, the flash of claws, a soft thud — and the rabbit was gone. Blotted beneath the furred weight, it struggled for an instant, its baby shriek slicing the glade with terror.

Leaping to her feet, Lenny screamed, "No! No!" But the rabbit hung broken in the cat's mouth with the kitten, on hind legs, already chewing on a lifeless paw. Then, just as quickly as it had happened there was nothing but an empty glade — and Lenny's foolish protest going on and on.

"Cut it out," Todd insisted. "Somebody will hear you."

"That's all you care?"

"Wow!" he exulted. "Whatta tackle! That cat should be on the team!"

Lenny stared in disbelief. Todd didn't care! He didn't care that the glade in one dreadful instant had become a place of death: death lurking in the shadows, slithering in the grass, waiting evil-eyed in the dark. For Lenny, beauty had turned to ugliness and love to hate. Sickened, she looked at Todd sprawled on the emerald moss and grinning in the white light. I hate him! she thought furiously.

"Hey! Where're you going?"

"Home," she grated between her teeth.

"Lenny!" he called as she thrashed into the bush.

Home! she thought despairingly as she burst onto the main path. How can I call the Blooms' place "home" when it's only somewhere between houses? Nothing! Absolutely nothing was the way it should be.

Nevertheless, the little house looked good, nestled in the hollow with Soapy on the lighted porch. The dog's ears pricked and his tail waved in welcome. Looking so like the old Soapy, Lenny thought, that I can hardly bear it.

On her knees, arms circling the dog's ruff, she moaned, "Oh, Soapy! Don't ever die!" And with the tears came the certain knowledge that she cried not only for Soapy, but for everything that came to an end.

Soapy coughed politely and Lenny loosened her hold. The dog padded quietly down the path to where Todd was leaning on the gate. "Hi, fella," he said. "Don't sound the alarm. It's only me."

If Todd opens that gate! Lenny thought. But he simply stood there, hands on the pickets, waiting. The yellow porch-light softened his bigness, making him appear suddenly very young. To Lenny he looked just like a little boy peering in a neighbour's window — not knowing whether he'd be punished or exactly what he'd find.

"Lenny?"

"Here," she said, walking slowly to meet him and stopping a deliberate foot from the fence.

"In the glade," he asked. "What did I do?"

"You spoiled it," she said, bitterly. "You got a real charge out of seeing something die."

His hands shot out, closing hard on her shoulders. "Wrong!" he told her. "I don't like death any more than you do. But back there, it made sense. Those cats have to eat. If they don't — *they die.*"

When she did not answer, he shook her roughly. "Can't you see it makes sense?"

She looked at him coldly. "Sense?"

"It *has* to," was the unsteady reply. "Have you ever seen a *man* die? I did — my own Dad — of a heart attack in the front hall. Can you beat it?"

The unexpected confession, the knowledge that Todd, too, was uncertain, maybe even afraid, released a flood of sympathy in Lenny. On impulse, she leaned forward, her kiss meant only to console. But his lips asked for more, clinging fiercely. And Lenny gave what she could. Because it's tonight, she thought. Clearly I can. Tonight, there's a fence in-between!

Todd drew away first and Lenny was embarrassed that he had to. Apart, they became instant strangers. He was Todd Adams of Ipperwash — and she was Lenny O'Hare of the Blooms'.

With a nonchalant, "Thanks, baby. That *did* make sense," he turned on his heel.

With a flippant, "Glad you liked it," Lenny raced Soapy to the porch.

Flicking off the light, tiptoeing breathless through the hall, she caught a faint glow from the kitchen, the clink of glass on glass.

Illumined by the open refrigerator, Gramps appeared in the doorway. Breadknife in one hand, a salami chub in the other, he whispered, "Hungry?"

"Famished," Lenny replied, and meant it. I love you, Gramps, she thought fervently. Funny, puckered old face, skinny old man in baggy pyjamas, you right my mixed-up world.

Later, in bed and on the fringes of sleep, Lenny admitted with reluctance that Ringo must be gone for good. The kitten she had seen, both this afternoon and tonight, was certainly not Ringo. It was a bobcat kitten, she concluded, and was never anything else.

But that first ime in the orchard, she could have sworn it was Ringo. Lenny closed her mind to the fact that bobcats and barn cats are not exactly friendly. Somewhere, she decided drowsily, Ringo is alive and well. Maybe in sombody's cottage. With that loud voice and having such a personality. . .!

16 Preparations

The week slipped smoothly away, each day a fun-day with Todd, each day a dazzle of sun.

But this morning dawned sunless, the sky looking remarkably like old porridge. Pressing into the pillow, Lenny snuggled the blanket closer, savouring its warmth on her aching legs. Aching legs? Oh, no! Not on Debra's birthday — the night of the big bonfire and the Yacht Club dance.

Swinging her legs free of the covers, Lenny recalled when, once before, she had raged aloud about the inconvenience of being female. "Think of your body as a nest," Mom had said, "being readied for the proper time. This," she had concluded with a smile, "is only a monthly housecleaning."

"Some nest!" Lenny muttered, meeting her own shadowed eyes in the mirror. A bit of make-up, though, could do wonders — and maybe an aspirin.

But a short search in her cosmetic case revealed only an empty bottle. She could have sworn she had thrown the empty one away and packed a new bottle in the pocket. Gram, of course, would have aspirin, but Lenny preferred not to ask. It meant confessing to something too personal, something she had just learned to bear. Older women, like Mom and Gram, always gave such superior sympathy. As if being fifteen is *my* fault!

On the stairs, Lenny was met by the sugar-sweet smell of baking angel cake. Gram must be making her specialty for Debra's party.

Replying half-heartedly to Gram's cheery greeting, Lenny

asked, "Would you have an aspirin?" And there it was again: Gram's searching look, the instant knowledge, the uncovering of Lenny's own secret.

"Why no, dear. I never take pills."

Oh, great! Lenny thought. But Gram, reaching behind the kitchen curtain, took from the sill a small labelled bottle. "A few drops of peppermint," she said briskly, "will mend your troubles."

Lenny didn't think so. The glass, half-filled with warm water, was spiked with a vile-smelling stuff. But with Gram watching, she downed it, exaggerating the shudder.

Gram, it seemed, was in no immediate need of Lenny's company. Bustling from table to oven, cheeks flushed and eyes bright, she looked disgustingly healthy. Now that she's poisoned me, Lenny thought, she can get on with her baking!

Huddling in a dimity duster, bare feet hooked on a chair rung, Lenny listened to the rain, the elm bending in a sudden gust and spattering the pane with spray. "Boy!" she remarked. "What a day for a party! Soggy bonfire! Soggy dance!"

But her remark echoed in an empty kitchen. Gram was upstairs, opening a closet door, coming down again with a tartan dressing gown and a pair of carpet slippers. "Here," she said. "These are Sid's. You'd better put them on. This is no time to catch cold." Stopping Lenny's argument before it began, she added. "There's no one to care what you wear."

Gramps, though, coming in the back door, shaking the wet from his hat, remarked, "What's wrong? Lenny sick or something?"

Miraculously, Lenny wasn't sick. The dull ache gone, her stomach clamoured for breakfast. "Nope," she told him brightly. "I'm waiting to pour your coffee."

Gramps scratched his head. "Well, now," he drawled. "You think you can make it the way I like?"

Lenny laughed. "Aw, c'mon, Gramps. Live dangerously." Handing him the cup, she waited while he sipped noisily.

"Okay?"

"Perfect," he said. "Going to be a perfect day, too. Just had to iron out a few kinks."

Like me, Lenny thought, catching the sparkle of one last trickle as it wandered to the sill.

"Got some mail, Gramps announced. "Barney Mann dropped it off at the dock. There's a letter for you, Lenny."

"Where?"

"Raincoat pocket. That Mann kid," he went on, "looked a mess. Up all night, I'll bet."

Lenny barely heard, rummaging in the damp pocket and leafing through farm folders. Then, the envelope with Dad's fly-away writing, " 'Scuse, please," she said, and ripped it open.

Dear Woodsy Kid:

New York is hotter than Hades! Wish we had an air-conditioned motel. But, nothing can compare with Black Rock Lake. Sure would like to be there with you.

Me too, Lenny thought, feeling a sudden pang.

While I tramp the pavement from one publisher to the next, your mother spends most of her time window-shopping. Getting ideas, she says, for new clothes for you.

Oh Mom! What about yourself?

The letter broke off, then began again with a new date. In block print, the one word *HALLELUJAH*! leaped from the page. *There's a good chance I might become contributing editor for a new trade publication called* Table D'hote — *Canadian branch. The magazine slants solely at the restaurant table. You know — colour scheme, cutlery, tableware, etc., etc. One thing nice, the O'Hare's will always eat! When Pop's on assignment, we're welcome in any restaurant in the city. We might even have to watch our waistlines!*

Lenny giggled, picturing three pudgy people waddling from steakhouse to steakhouse.

"Good news?" Gramps asked.

Lenny beamed. "Daddy thinks he might be an editor for a magazine. They're coming home," — she checked with the letter — "on July 25 — that's tomorrow! And they'll meet me if I take the 7 p.m. bus."

"They'd love to come up to the lake." she added. "But they want to find a house. Get settled before school starts." A white square fluttered to the floor and Gram retrieved it. "A snapshot," she said.

"Mom and Dad!" Lenny exclaimed. Her parents, arm-in-arm in front of Macy's store, laughed into the camera.

Over Lenny's shoulder, Gramps remarked. "Your mother looks as young as her daughter."

It was true; by some trick of light, every line was smoothed from Mom's face. Chin thrown high, she looked younger than Lenny could recall; carefree and happy. Dad's smile, though, looked stiff. *"Free lancing,"* he had written, *"will be out. I'll have to forget about my precious book for a while."* He won't like that, Lenny decided. Dad loves that book more than anything. But *not* more than Mom! was her exultant conclusion.

"Isn't it terrific!" Lenny cried.

"Terrific," Gram agreed, the word sounding strange on her lips. But the meaning remained the same. Mom and Dad were coming home together. There was no danger of separation!

The oven-timer clinked, and Gram went to her cake. Three cakes, Lenny noted, graded in size and tinted a golden brown. Lifting them carefully from stove to table, Gram suspended each one bottom-side-up, their funnels perched precariously on upturned glasses. "Don't anyone stomp in this kitchen," she commanded.

"Could I do anything to help?" Lenny asked.

"Yes," Gram said. "You can deliver the cake to the Brewsters'. But not right away. It has to hang while it cools. And then there's the icing."

"You going to trust this girl with your masterpiece?" Gramps teased.

"Lenny will be careful," Gram replied.

"I won't even breathe on it," Lenny assured her.

Leaping to her feet, above the whirr of Gram's beater, Lenny shouted, "I'd better get dressed."

" 'S about time!" Gramps shouted back.

"Now Sid," Gram admonished. "The child has a right to sit about in a dressing gown. She's feeling poorly today."

Lenny didn't wait to hear what else Gram had to say. Tripping over Gramps's bulky gown, she stumbled happily up the stairs. I'm just a l'il old nest, she thought crazily.

"You sure as heck are," she told the untidy vision in the mirror.

Two hours later, with the chores done, Lenny waited on the front walk while Gram gently lowered the birthday cake into the carton fitted snugly on the small wagon and taped strips of clear wrap over the carton's top.

"It's the dreamiest cake I've ever seen," Lenny declared.

"I do my best," Gram said modestly.

Gram's best was a three-tiered confection, tinted a delicate yellow and necklaced with spun-sugar flowers.

"Pretty delivery-girl," Gramps remarked. "What happened to the frump in the kitchen?"

Work, Lenny could have told him, and a bit of imagination to change dull, determined curls into shoulder-length shine, and a touch of light and shadow to make her eyes a wider blue. Plus a new top to match her last clean shorts.

"I do my best," she mimicked, starting off with a laugh.

The sun slanted hazily on the "low" path as Lenny walked slowly backward, easing the wagon over the stones. A chipmunk hyphened up the trail, a tiny black-brown streak. Swinging on a rainbow thread, a spider patched a dew-heavy web. And near the upturned tree-roots, some fireweed had burst its pods, silky tufts bearing tiny seeds. Always, Lenny thought, the weed follows fire. So maybe, long ago, the steps in the glade *did* lead somewhere. Maybe fire had simply swept it clean.

"Gotcha!" Barney said, and Lenny jumped with fear.

"Idiot!" she screamed. "Look what you've done!" The jolt had tilted the carton and flattened some flowers on the cake.

Bending to inspect the damage, and dropping the handle on Barney's bare foot as she did so, Lenny wailed, "After all Gram's work!"

"You've mashed my foot," he replied mildly.

"Why" Lenny demanded angrily, "do you always ruin things?"

"Maybe," he said in a low voice, "because I'm good at it."

She looked at him closely, and he lowered his eyes, peering with exaggerated concern at the two crushed flowers. But not before Lenny caught his tired resignation — and something almost like hurt.

"Sorry about this," he mumbled. "I'll explain to Mrs. Brewster."

"I'm sorry, too," Lenny admitted. "I shouldn't have blown my top. You scared me, that's all."

"Three times I've scared you," was the wry reminder. He picked up the wagon handle and started down the path, Lenny steadying the carton from the rear. "That's what I came to tell you," he said. "That you won't be shot at again. At least, not by me." His back was stiff and Lenny remained silent.

"This morning," he announced, "I went to the Forest Rangers and told them what happened. Got a fine, my gun confiscated — and a warning."

Without turning, he added. "Lenny, so help me! I honestly thought you were a bobcat. I never meant . . . ."

"I should never have been there," she interrupted. "It was a crazy place to be."

Barney's bare shoulders straightened and the wagon surged ahead.

"Hey!" she warned. "Watch it!"

"You don't trust me?"

"Oh sure," she agreed dubiously, one eye on the jiggling cake. A battered birthday cake, she thought, was hardly the way to start a celebration. And tonight had to be special. Tonight was the last one at the lake.

Delivery of the cake completed, Lenny and Barney were relieved of their responsibility. Debra, though, spotted the crushed flowers immediately.

115

"Well?" she asked.

"Accident," he said.

"It figures," Debra quipped, not asking for an explanation. She's marvellous for Barney, Lenny thought.

"Happy Birthday," she said.

"Thanks," was the reply. "But it isn't official yet. Not till 9 o'clock."

"The exact time when Deb was born," Jill chipped in. "The time when we put a match to that."

"That" was a towering pile of brushwood on the small beach of the inlet. It was at least twenty feet in height and covered with a huge tarpaulin. Todd, in the same scarlet trunks, was struggling to free the pile of its protection.

"Hey!" he called. "Somebody lend a hand. This thing's going to topple."

"You go, Lenny," Debra said.

"What's wrong with me?" Barney demanded.

"You and I," he was told, "are going daisy-picking. Tonight we're going Hawaiian. Leis, guitars, the works. The daisies are for leis."

Barney's groan followed Lenny down to the beach. "Daisy-picking? A big boy like me?"

Still laughing, she greeted Todd's smile with, "Hi! I'm your extra hand."

The tarpaulin proved more of a problem than they expected. Caught on a high twig, it threatened to collapse the whole pile. Not until they had commandeered two ladders was the unveiling successful. Even so Lenny lost her balance and did a prat-fall in the sand. Flat on her back and helpless with laughter, she lay there with Todd standing over her. I'll remember him always she thought, just like this, longlegged and brown, blond head rimmed against the sky.

"Time for a swim," he said. "C'mon."

"Not today," she said quickly.

Without asking "Why?" he turned, splashed through the shallows, and churned swiftly out into the lake. Todd *knows*, she

116

thought with surprise. And he didn't persist.

Somehow, the shared knowledge was a warm and tender thing — a good thing — making her feel tremendously important.

17 Beach Party

Throughout the sun-yellow day, the feeling of importance continued, not just for Lenny herself, but for all that this last day contained: every moment too filled with happy preparation to feel sadness because it would end.

Crowded in the Brewster kitchen, they perched on stools wielding melon-ballers and scooping out pineapples. Todd, coming in hot and dishevelled, announced that he had finally found three punts. "You and your great ideas!" he said to Debra. "Boat-bottoms for tables, yet!"

Barney clucked his tongue. "Join the chain gang," he sympathized.

"You call *that* work?" Todd asked, pointing at Barney's pile of melon balls.

Grinning, Barney shot back, "Cool off, boy. Have a ball on the house." The ball, a perfect shot, splashed on Todd's bare chest leaving a trail of mush. In all the noise and the ensuing scuffle, Lenny came to an unexpected decision: I could *like* Barney Mann, she thought.

Then came a quiet time on the beach with waves lip-lipping the shore while they helped Mrs. Brewster and Mrs. Mann.

Too busy to bother with words, Gerry and Jill poked neat holes in bait cans to make storm lanterns. Barney and his mother, surrounded by lamp chimneys, polished each one with care, replacing old wicks and filling the lamps with fuel. Dark heads bent over a common task, they looked, for one brief moment, relaxed and free of trouble.

Todd and Lenny sprayed glitter on the chimneys while Mrs. Brewster and Debra lit candles, dripping the wax in the bait cans to hold the candles upright. None of it was very important, yet the feeling of importance persisted: a quiet, happy time when everyone worked together. Debra, Lenny mused, was not Mrs. Brewster's daughter — only her stepdaughter. But surely Todd must realize that money was his mother's *last* reason for marriage to Debra's father. Money helped. But it wasn't everything.

Sitting a few feet distant, Lenny caught their exchanged smiles. Then she smiled, herself — at no one in particular.

That evening, dinner seemed unnecessary. Despite Gram's good cooking, Lenny had to refuse it.

"Where's your appetite, girl?" Gramps demanded.

"She's too excited," Gram chided. "Besides, she'll be having supper at sunset. Go along, Lenny. You'll want to get ready for the dance."

With a grateful "thanks," Lenny left the table, hearing Gramps's protest, "Whatta waste!" and his wife's reminder that he seemed to have forgotten how it was to be young. The idea that Gram and Gramps had once been young was completely new, an idea which Lenny had never considered. They're also rich, she told herself. And they couldn't care less. How wrong can a person be about others, she wondered. Looks and actions didn't always count.

Later, viewing herself critically in the mirror, Lenny could almost see the reflection of her own radiance. Shining hair, for once, obediently straight, framed a clear-skinned face. Her dress with its outsize sunflower climbing from a brief hem was a product of Mom's patient sewing. Deceptively simple, it clung to hips and breast, its colour making Lenny's eyes a deeper hue. "Fantastic," she breathed happily. "Simply great."

But, for some reason, maybe because this day was her last, it was also a time for being honest. Reluctantly, she admitted that the wide blue eyes were not entirely her own. They were a gift from Dad — along with his easy laughter. And the dark hair was Mother's contribution — added to her love for beauty and the need to hold it close.

"Please," Lenny prayed aloud to this image, this combination of blue-eyed and dark-haired need. "Please let Dad get the job, always able to laugh — and have Mom to believe."

Turning her back on the mirror, she headed for the bedroom window.

"Hey!" Todd called from the front walk. "You got company?"

Not sure which was more splendid — Todd, or the horizon — Lenny simply stared. The sky, lavender beneath clear blue, unveiled a perfect sunset. Todd, in white shirt and yachting jacket, had already reached perfection!

Neither had seen the other in anything but beachwear and for a moment they were speechless.

"Wow!" Todd said, breaking the spell.

"Be right down," Lenny told him, snatching a purse from the chair.

On the path, hurrying past the fallen tree, Lenny felt a fleeting sadness, the small, fervent wish that Debra could have been born on some other night. Tonight, she thought wistfully, should've been reserved for a special "good-bye."

"Where's the fire?" she panted. Todd, misunderstanding, replied, "We left the pile on the beach. Remember?"

Bypassing Ipperwash with its lights and laughter, they followed the trail to the beach where Debra received her guests. Seated on inflated air mattresses were the familiar "six," faces blooming in the flicker of lanterns.

The three punts draped in vivid canvas — red, blue and orange — now served as tables. On them, copper chafing dishes held glazed drumsticks and sweet n' sour meatballs. And summer fruits glowed in heaps of juicy delight. A feast, Lenny thought, too beautiful to eat.

Daisies were everywhere! Debra and Barney had gathered armfuls and saved them in the fridge. Now, spilling from basket and bottle, they made a carpet for the centre table and Debra's birthday cake.

A wood sprite in emerald green, Debra stood on tiptoe to garland Lenny's neck. "Your lei," she said. "Welcome to the blue lagoon."

"Thanks," Lenny said. "And many happy returns." There was a small, panic-filled moment when she wondered if Debra really meant her previous command, "No presents." But there were no packaged gifts in sight, so Lenny breathed more easily.

"I told you," Debra was saying, "my birthday's only an excuse." She waved in the direction of the house where guests spilled from the veranda and sauntered toward the beach. Lenny felt a twinge of sympathy, but her hostess fluttered away, busying herself with other things. Todd too, after finding Lenny a seat, left her with the remark, "Better make myself useful."

At her side, Barney asked, "This your last night, Lenny?"

Mutely she nodded, eyes on Todd and face-to-face with the hurt of saying "good-bye."

Barney understood. "Todd'll be around," he assured her. "You can bet on it."

"When?" she asked miserably. "He's going East, to school."

"Look," he said. "This is a party — not a funeral."

Lenny did not answer. And Barney, nipping a daisy from his lei, perched it behind Lenny's ear. "Nice," he said.

"Hey, you!" Todd called. "Quit making time with my gal. And bring me some matches. It's fire-lighting time."

The hot, orange glare of the fire, the circle of rose-tinted faces, the hands twined in auld-lang-syne — all combined to give Lenny a feeling of belonging — and at the same time of not belonging.

Suddenly lonely, she looked around and found her eyes linked with Barney's. She smiled. And the surprising reminder came that a month ago she would not have been caught dead with Barney Mann!

The Yacht Club perched high above the lake, its spotlights greening the terraced lawns and whitening the zig-zag of railings. Climbing the steps, crossing the spacious sun-deck and entering the powder room with its ceiling-high mirrors, Lenny felt increasingly ill-at-ease. *I've never been to a Yacht Club before. I won't know how to act*!

Mary, in gossamer-white, blonde hair brushed high, seemed to blend with the white-gold room. Deb too, in her emerald outfit, belonged.

"Well?" Lenny asked herself pertly. "Do we stay here all night? To play 'mirror on the wall'?"

She giggled. Nowhere could there be three more different girls. A princess in white. A leprechaun in green. And a dark-haired prop for one sunflower. That, of course, was the answer. I'll never be a leprechaun — nor a princess. But I *can* be Lenny O'Hare. It was that simple.

"Let's go," she said.

As Lenny O'Hare, she enjoyed the Yacht Club Dance, partnered now with Todd, now with Barney. Laughing, she asked him, "What was all that jazz about a mashed foot?"

"I told you," Barney said. "Anything I do well — I do often. Like messing things up — and dancing."

"There's a difference."

"What's that?"

"Those other times weren't for real."

One dark brow rose in a now-familiar peak. "How did you know?" he asked.

"I didn't," she told him. "I just this minute found out."

Later, at intermission, Lenny and Todd leaned on the sun-deck railing. The lake, veiled in fog, had lost its sparkle, tall pines rick-racking the far shore.

Arm round her shoulders, he snuggled her close. "Tonight," he said, "will have to be 'good-bye.' "

"Now!"

He nodded. "Tomorrow I promised to run the Camp cruiser. The skipper's sick and there's a bunch of kids expected. I won't be able to see you off."

Drowning in disappointment, Lenny was silent. But Todd, reaching with thumb and forefinger, squeezed her chin. "I won't forget you, Lenny O'Hare," he said, and kissed her on the lips.

They promised each other letters — and next summer at the

lake.

"Next summer," Lenny echoed.

"At the lake," Todd whispered.

Then he added mischievously, "We can even take a run up Satan's Gorge again."

Hand in hand they went back to the dance.